C000125880

Incognito

ISBN 9798634795737

Independently published.

www.michaelwinson.com

For the woman that makes it all worth it, my amazing Wife.

And for my boys. You can do anything you set out to.

I'm proud of you all.

Incognito

By

Michael Winson

CHAPTER 1 – ABDUL

Blending in was easier than he expected. The trick was to allow himself to be carried on the current of people around him, thousands of them, all aimlessly walking in the same direction, all unaware of the deadly plan that he would soon bring to life.

He practically disappeared, swallowed up by the hordes. There was nothing more obvious than one person going against a crowd. Next to screaming 'Allahu Akbar' at the top of his lungs and waving a trigger in his hand, nothing would make it more obvious that he was *not* just another one of the oblivious crowd of shoppers, walking around the Trafford Centre on this busy Saturday morning, than moving against the tide.

It struck him that there was a serenity to being part of the herd. The way that everyone seemed to know, without being told, that they must move in a certain direction, how there were no obvious altercations or differences in what the people passing around him wanted to do. Everyone blindly followed the invisible arrows that directed them to spend their money and then, no doubt, tweet about it so that others felt compelled to do the same.

He stopped to browse the window of the Breitling store. Cases upon cases of shining precious metal straps, and diamond encrusted watch faces, reflected the lights from above, reminding him of treasure chests from the pirate movies he loved when he was young.

Through the cases he could see a young man, twenty-something, heading to the door carrying a fancy box suggesting he'd made an extravagant purchase. He wondered how the man could seem so happy about being part of a system that placed value only on his money. Would he regret his greed, when he was away from the fawning young girl on his other arm, that he must be so desperate to impress? Had he found a way to justify such avarice when he was alone with only his thoughts for company?

Abdul moved away from the window and followed the tide of people, and the young couple, to the Kurt Geiger shop next door. The couple entered and he stopped outside the window again, watching the same young playboy head directly to what was clearly the most expensive section of the shop, marked, for all to see, by a different style of décor; thick pile carpeting was laid in this section of the floor, three different shades of leather adorned the wall panels, where elsewhere there was only cheap wood laminate.

The young man that had caught Abdul's attention was clearly in a hurry to complement the new beacon of excess he'd bought for his wrist with some new shoes. So much of a hurry that he barged past an elderly woman, who was leaning forwards inspecting a pair of brown leather sandals, knocking her sideways. She did well to grab the shelving unit in time to keep herself upright. He didn't stop. He didn't look back.

It was clear, in that one act, that the man he'd been watching had no humanity. He wasn't the least bit bothered that he'd almost hurt one of the elders of his society. His only interests, Abdul thought, were money and status, like so many others.

It was also clear in that moment that he, Abdul Azim, 'Servant of the Mighty' in the language of non-believers, was in the right place, and that the mission he and the rest of the Brotherhood were on today had been well selected. They were going to strike at the heart of all that was important in this society.

CHAPTER 2 – LISA

The heat in the room was stifling. The feeling of hair sticking to the back of her neck made it almost oppressive. She swept the hair back, away from her neck, gathering it with both hands into a tight ponytail at the back of her head, deftly pulling the elastic-band that she always wore on her right wrist over her hand. She snapped the band off her wrist, around the fistful of hair, securing it in place.

Every couple of months she debated cutting her hair shorter. A purely practical choice that meant she could save herself an hour a day by not having to go through the torturous routine of straightening her hair. If she didn't, it dried thick and curly, a look she hated despite only ever getting compliments on the rare occasion she had been caught short for time.

Every visit to the hairdresser, once a month religiously, she came up with a reason *not* to shorten it. She had a list of good reasons, but the main one was that she worried it'd make her look like she did in the photos from her childhood, when her parents had made her style choices for her. When neighbours in her street thought, for at least four years, that the Reid family had two boys for children, not a boy and a girl.

One day she supposed she would have to forgive her parents. Maybe even thank them. Being a girl with a bowl cut made it difficult to be one of the 'girlie' girls in her formative years. She knew that she wouldn't have enjoyed that. As a child she never wanted to be a princess and couldn't stand Disney. Her childhood had been about riding bikes and climbing trees. Competing with the boys. Things like that stuck with you for life.

As she got older, she naturally became more aware of her femininity, but that competitive spirit stayed with her.

In her teenage years, her hair became her main source of rebellion. She dyed it all sorts of colours, knowing it would piss off her Mum and Dad. It became a sport after a while, testing how far she could go before she got a bite from them. Even now, at the age of thirty-one, there was a slight red tinge to her otherwise brunette ponytail, left over from when she'd had it coloured a month ago.

The warmth on the back of her neck made her reach for that ponytail now. Splitting it in to two strands and pulling, making sure it was tight as it could be. With this heat she didn't need it coming loose.

There were so many monitors, computers and extra bodies in the security control room of the Trafford Centre, with no air conditioning to cool the fifteen-foot-long by eight-foot wide space, that it was never going to be cold.

There was no getting away from it and no point in complaining. She was stuck here until the job was done, one way or another.

That didn't bother Lisa. Needs must when the stakes were high. Somebody in this building might have information on the most dangerous terrorist on the planet, and Lisa was going to find out for sure.

CHAPTER 3 – ABDUL

The shopping centre had over two hundred stores, with nearly two million square feet of shop space, and over three miles of walkways linking them all as part of an interconnecting concourse.

Even at 9.30am, when Abdul drove up to the building, it was tough to find a space in the car park that was built to house almost twelve thousand vehicles. That was over an hour ago. He was confident it would be overflowing by now, with traffic snarled up as a result. A bonus as far as his mission goes.

He had seen countless times how eager Mancunians, fighting to merge their cars into single file traffic, would get so close to each other, stubbornly refusing to give up their place in the queue for anyone or anything, emergency vehicles included.

That was only the car drivers. Buses were very popular in Manchester and they were scheduled to drop full loads of shoppers and socialisers at the centre every fifteen minutes.

There was a steady stream of people already walking in the direction of the centre as he drove in that morning. The rain helped. It rained more frequently in Manchester than anywhere he'd ever known. Something about the hills that surrounded the area he had been told as a kid. It seemed to always be raining.

Today that was good. Everybody would be looking for indoor options to commit their time to, which meant a lot of people choosing shopping. Abdul thought that there would be as many as a quarter of a million people passing through the doors of the Trafford Centre today.

How many might get out again was a very different number.

He thought briefly of the rest of the Brotherhood, all blending in at strategic points around this massive building. He wondered if they too had their resolve strengthened by examples of inhumanity like he had seen.

He wanted to change route, to stay close to the pillar that was to be his starting position when the time came. Simply turning about-face and walking in the opposite direction was not an option. That could easily be spotted by some keen-eyed security guard. Ever since the devastation of 9/11 and the 7/7 terror attacks in London, the number of CCTV cameras in the UK had increased more than ten-fold. There were plenty of them in this building, covering every inch of floor space, looking for anything out of place.

Abdul turned his head ninety degrees to the left and then the right. To anyone else he looked like he was searching for the next shop on his route, but in fact he was checking for camera positions. There were five in his immediate view, and more behind him that he had seen earlier, as well as those mounted inside the shops themselves. Seeing this he felt some satisfaction that he was right to stress the point in their planning meetings.

Some of the Brothers had been less concerned with the risk that CCTV posed to their mission. They were convinced that the chaos and uncertainty brought about by Brexit, and the shambolic state of the British government since, had more than distracted the public from the vigilance that they used to have for potential attacks.

They may have been right. Abdul knew first-hand how fickle the British could be. Especially on a day like today, the first of a three-day holiday weekend, where most people would be lost in their own plans of how to spend their extra day off work.

None of that mattered to the plan. No matter what else might be at play, today was not the day for taking risks.

What was about to unfold in this building was the culmination of a lifetime of planning, and something as small as one misplaced glance or obvious change of direction threatened to derail everything that they had worked for.

Now that the day had come, Abdul had to keep that at the forefront of his mind. It wasn't easy.

Images of the people he'd lost were constantly in his thoughts today. They were never *not* there, but over time he'd been able to push them far enough to the edge of conscious thought to dull the pain. Abdul knew that if he allowed the pain in, it would paralyze him. Again. Today was not the day for that. Today would be his permanent painkilling solution. He needed to focus. To hold out long enough to get his job done.

The atmosphere in the walkway was like a party. The crowds were bustling. Each voice fought to be heard over the music system that pumped generic pop music around the building and kept the crowds moving along.

A group of four teenage girls walked by Abdul, three of them singing along to the Katy Perry track that was playing, while the fourth filmed the whole thing in selfie mode on her mobile phone. He allowed himself a smile and the girl closest to him smiled back at him. She couldn't have known the reason he was smiling was because he found it fascinating, and hilarious, how young girls now seemed to all look the same.

He could have guessed how this group would look before they came into view. Each with their hair tied back and up, tight to their heads, ponytails swishing like actual horse tails as they turned and talked to each other. Their tops were minimal, showing as much midriff as they could get away with and amplifying cleavage. Jeans looked like they'd been painted on rather than being worn, with slashes and slits all up the legs. The more daring of the girls sporting the biggest holes in their jeans.

In any group of girls Abdul knew there were two constant truths. The lads he used to play football with had taught him about them. Rule one; there always one girl who, the other girls would never admit but secretly knew, was only in the group because she didn't quite fit the mould of the others and so made the others look more attractive. Rule two; in any group there was always one that went further than the others, sexually.

11

The lads had told stories of the successes they'd had by targeting the girl in a group that dressed more daringly than the others. They swore it meant that she was the one most likely to put out.

Abdul wasn't interested in girls like that. He wasn't interested in girls at all today. His gaze came back to their faces, and their make-up. What was it with the make-up? Eyebrows that were clearly not natural, but instead looked like they'd been drawn on, using a masonry brush.

In Abdul's schooldays they'd have been bullied heavily for wearing those caterpillars on their faces. Maybe things had changed, or maybe the impact of them was lessened with every layer of fake tan that was applied. That thought was the one that made him smile the most.

As his eyes moved across the line of four, the shade of orange became more and more pronounced, like a decorator's colour chart. As he anticipated, the girl closest to him, her skin a shade below mahogany in most visible places, fingers marks obvious where she'd done a bad job of self-applying the tan to her arms, also had the most rips in her jeans. He could see the entire lining of her pockets poking out through holes that were practically at crotch level.

Maybe the lads had it wrong, maybe it was the grading of fake tan that determined promiscuity levels and not the way they dressed. Whatever the measure, in the example in front of him right now, Mahogany had it won by a good margin on both counts.

Abdul turned his back to the phone camera as Mahogany drew level with him, still singing about kissing a girl and liking it. He knew about facial recognition software. He'd seen plenty of police procedural shows on TV. He made every effort over the years to not stand out. He was always clean shaven with a short back and sides haircut. Five feet and ten inches tall and a thirty-two-inch waist, the only thing that marked him as different to anyone else was his Middle Eastern complexion, and here in Manchester with its melting pot culture even that wasn't very different. The only word to describe his appearance was average.

Above average when it came to smarts, he didn't see a benefit in being featured in Mahogany's Instagram story.

Thinking of avoiding the camera on her phone, he walked into JD King of Trainers next to Kurt Geiger. He wanted to change direction and it was much easier to do that unnoticed when coming out of a shop. As well as the practical benefit, he needed some respite from the noise of the crowds. He felt tension coursing through him. This day had been on his mind for a very long time. As the past months and days had been counting down, he'd found himself struggling to sleep.

A nervous energy he couldn't quite explain, and hadn't shared with anyone for fear of having to try, had been waking him at around 3am every morning. The headaches came soon afterwards, from overthinking things most likely. Starting as a once a week annoyance, they had quickly ramped up to a once a day plague. Until recently he'd never taken any regular medication. Today was different. He knew he shouldn't be taking so many. He'd washed down eight already this morning and had another full bottle in his pocket if needed. They were only over the counter paracetamol, but even so he knew taking that many pills in a short space of time could be dangerous. He figured it was a risk worth taking to shift the headaches for today, and he wasn't exactly worried about his long-term health.

His heart thumped like he'd just finished a half marathon. The beat of his pulse in his ears so loud that he could barely hear the spotty teenager in the store ask him if needed any help. He didn't need to hear him. He knew the drill. He'd been here lots of times over the last few months to check out the building and security around his position. It was obvious that all the staff in this shop had the same script to work from when someone came in.

Abdul politely thanked the Assistant and told him he'd call him over if he needed anything. He headed over to the new Nike display shelf on the back wall.

Abdul was blessed with a young complexion. With the right clothing and his natural accent, having spent most of his young life in Heywood, a small town halfway between Bury and Rochdale, just eight miles north of the

Trafford Centre, he could pass himself off for just another flash twenty-something lad looking for the latest trainers.

He'd planned for exactly this when he came on a recce to the centre the month before, coming into this same shop to pick up the new pair of Nike Air Force Ones he wore today, along with the Quest jacket that he was also sporting. It wasn't his usual style. Normally he preferred dark and neutral colours that matched his preference to blend in. This jacket was far too bright for that, with its green, pink, and yellow coloured panels and pockets. Not to mention the hundred-and-eighty-pound price tag that came along with it. He'd never spent more than thirty pounds on one item of clothing before, and he'd felt wasteful doing it for this one jacket. Wearing something so expensive, and awful to look at, was a first for him.

He had to look past all that this time. The oversize design gave it a practicality that more than made up for the gaudy colouring. It easily allowed him to cover the bulk of the vest that he was wearing underneath, and the variety of different sized pockets that the jacket provided was perfect for his needs.

Although the Brotherhood were devoted in faith, each abandoned the traditional garments and style that were synonymous with their faith, for the higher purpose of going unnoticed in a crowd. They always dressed and groomed to match their surroundings. The City of Manchester had one of the largest Islamic communities in the UK, but the Brotherhood was not formed to hide amongst their own. It was formed to operate in the world of the infidels. To take the fight to them in the places that they held most dear. The Brothers kept their hair short. Their beards were trimmed neatly or were clean shaven. The purpose was to appear, to anyone outside their circle, like any other young British man.

Since a child, Abdul was a natural at not being noticed. Bullying in Manchester schools taught him that lesson very quickly.

The staff and customers in the trainer shop paid him no more attention and, after picking up and inspecting trainers for 5 minutes, he left the shop, turned right, and headed back to his pillar.

Katy Perry has been replaced by Ed Sheeran on the speaker system. Abdul thought the guitar that Ed strummed was much easier on the ears. He could still hear the thrumming of his pulse in his ears, but it was less urgent, and he could focus on the job he came here to do.

The only things on his mind were the cold metal touch of the trigger nestled in the right-hand pocket of his expensive windbreaker, the pregnant silence of the mobile phone in his left-hand pocket, and the number of people wandering the malls of the Trafford Centre.

Abdul looked around at the throngs of young shoppers and families that flooded the wide walkways as he casually headed back past the Breitling shop. He thought he might have been too conservative with his estimate of a quarter of a million people.

When the mobile phone in his pocket began vibrating, Abdul was snapped out of all thoughts except one; exactly how many of those people would not make it out of the fiery mess of mangled steel and crumbled concrete that this building was about to become.

CHAPTER 4 – LISA

Lisa regretted her outfit choice for the day. Outside of this room, the stretch-fit indigo blue jeans, loose-fitting white shirt and casual checked blazer, finished off with her trademark four-inch heels, was an outfit that made her feel confident. Lisa knew the shoes weren't a sensible choice, she also knew the power of dressing well.

She worked hard on her figure and her clothing choices deliberately accentuated the most potent parts of it. In her line of work, it made no sense to let an advantage go to waste.

In this room it was no advantage. She'd have been much cooler in something lighter and looser fitting. She would also feel less self-conscious. She could feel at least two sets of eyes on her as she eased back her shoulders, unintentionally pushing her chest forwards, to allow her blazer to slip away and try to get some relief from the heat. One pair belonged to one of the security guards. A young lad, he probably didn't have much experience with women, she thought. It was uncomfortable to know that he was watching her, but he was no threat.

The other pair she couldn't see but knew they'd be watching. Her partner Will was behind her and to the right, perched on the edge of a desk. He was the other reason she stuck with the high-heels instead of a more practical pair of pumps. It was an expensive habit. She often had to kick her heels off if she had to move fast, and more than a few times had returned to where she'd left a pair only to find them missing. Her taste in shoes wasn't cheap, but she knew that the jeans and heels combo drove Will crazy, and *that* was priceless. She didn't mind his eyes on her. She planned on it.

Lisa searched around for the water bottle she'd brought with her and found it on the edge of one of the control consoles. Despite the humid atmosphere in the control room, it retained some of the chill from the fridge she'd liberated it from and hadn't quite become undrinkable yet. Drinking deeply from it, she once more scanned the bank of fifteen monitors on the wall for signs of something, anything, unusual.

She'd been on site for three hours now and was starting to get the feeling that this was another wild goose chase. SO15, the counter terrorism arm of the British police service, seemed to get more of those than anything else.

Wasted efforts were more common now than ever and that was saying something for a service that, for over 20 years, got a tip-off every time someone spoke with an Irish accent.

Things had changed now. Lisa often thought, when she took the chance to stand back and look at the big picture, what a shame it was that people hadn't. Especially British people. Considering hers was a country with such a broad spectrum of citizens from all over the globe, she was amazed at how resilient xenophobia seemed to be.

Terrorism may be unrecognizable now from what it was in the seventies and eighties but, to a good portion of the country at least, bigotry remained a familiar friend.

A Muslim carrying a prayer mat now was as much a threat, to those people, as an Irishman carrying a grenade launcher was in the eighties.

It seemed to Lisa that most of her time was spent disproving crackpot tip-offs or investigating 'revenge tips'; the latest craze that had teenagers phoning or emailing in about someone they said was plotting an attack, as a way of getting back at them for perceived wrongdoing. Or worse, just for a laugh. What had happened to kids? Where had the magic that she saw when she looked back on her own childhood gone?

The last one of these tips had nearly cost her career, and a young man his life. Lisa was leading an early raid on a fourth floor flat on Moss Side. The suspect, Rafik Ansari, was flagged to them by a neighbour because of the large amounts of fertilizer being brought up to the flat over the space of a couple of days. It seemed perfectly viable as a lead; who needs twenty bags of fertilizer in a flat that has no garden and is forty feet from the ground?

Along with that bit of intelligence gold, the informant had also mentioned large bags of nails being part of the suspects shopping list.

The working theory was that a nail bomb was the most likely threat. Research into Rafik's social media activity suggested sympathy and increasing anger over the plight of Afghan and Syrian refugees. A common sign of possible radicalisation.

The intel had come through as top priority. In Lisa's world that meant there was no time for in-depth surveillance. The threat was imminent and had to be dealt with immediately. Her team were used to this. How many *non*-urgent terrorist threats were there?

They knew the drill well, having trained for it constantly in downtime between ops, but there was a complication of it being on the fourth floor; they could not breach multiple points of entry simultaneously, as they would in training. Other than a few officers on the ground, and four positioned on the external fire escapes, all of them had to funnel through a single point of entry at the front door.

On the stroke of 4.15am Lisa's team breached the front door of the flat. The reinforced steel ram made light work of the wooden front door. Taking it clean off the rusting hinges that held it to the weathered doorframe. Unusually, it didn't fly into the hallway of the flat as they'd expected. Instead it bounced outwards and knocked over the officer that was still recoiling from swinging the ram.

There was another barrier, a steel reinforced secondary door, fitted six inches behind the main door, mounted on a steel frame built into the inside walls so that it was flush. No hinges, handles or windows to be seen anywhere.

This kind of set up was rarer than the movies suggested. Nonetheless her team were trained for this and set to work on blowing the door open by placing shape charges - small explosives designed for highly targeted power with minimal collateral damage - at ten-inch intervals around the visible edge of the plain steel door.

It was impossible to tell, quickly enough, how a door like this might be mounted and where hinges, locks or bolts might be located on the other side, so the accepted approach was to target all possible combinations in one blast and keep the time taken to gain entry as short as possible.

Regardless of how prepared the team were, the presence of the barrier was enough to delay them by a couple of minutes. More than enough time for Rafik to be woken by the initial breach and react.

Once the steel door flew inwards from the explosion, Lisa could see a thick cloud of heavy smoke pouring out of the main living area, the first room on the right-hand side as she looked in from the entryway. She inched through the smoke, crouching low for better visibility, and spotted movement towards the back of the flat, through the kitchen door.

She shouted through the smoke 'Armed police, get down on the ground with your hands behind your head. Now!'

There was no response. Lisa got closer to the floor to get a better view under the growing smoke cloud. She could see a pair of legs scrambling for purchase on the lino of the kitchen floor, moving erratically as if the owner was trying to kick something high up in front of them. She shuffled forward as quickly as she could in the choking smoke, coughing heavily as she drew the foul-smelling smoke in to her lungs.

The team behind her could not risk moving ahead because of the poor visibility. They had no choice but to stay closely packed together in the entry funnel. Rather than get in each other's way, Lisa instructed them to break off into the rooms either side of the hallway and clear them as they went, leaving just her and her partner to clear the kitchen, the last room in the pokey flat.

She had to practically snake crawl to move forwards. The smoke was coming so fast and thick that to do anything else could be fatal from the fumes alone, never mind whatever weapons the suspect might have trained on them from the other side of the smog. The legs in front of her were still doing their strange 'one up, two down' dance. Clearly whatever was being kicked was stronger than the owner of the legs had expected.

She shouted again 'Last chance. If you don't get down on the floor with your hands behind your head right now, I *will* shoot.'

The legs stopped moving, slightly twisting from left to right. In her mind's eye Lisa saw the suspect turning left to right, looking around for something, anything to break through whatever he was trying to kick. A window she imagined. It could only be imagined, the smoke was settling, limiting her view to only the lower legs in front of her.

She heard the unmistakable sound of metal brushing against leather, like a sword being drawn by a knight entering in to battle. Instinctively she raised her firearm in front of her and steadied herself, rising to one knee to give her the best firing stance. As she saw the right leg begin to raise once more, her brain worked through the possible next steps quickly. Was he attempting another kick? Was he about to make an armed charge at her and her team? She decided she could not allow either thing to happen and fired two shots in quick succession.

The shots had to be fired at her own eye level or she'd have no way to judge how they'd landed. The first missed, punching a hole the size a tennis ball in the wall behind her target. The second hit just above the left knee. The hole it made wasn't as big this time, but the impact was greater. She saw the leg buckle and the foot slide to the left as the bullet ripped through. The right leg came back down, sliding wildly off to the right causing the suspect to perform an awkward version of the splits.

The guy screamed in pain as he desperately tried to retain balance. It was a pointless exercise. As his legs each went their own way, he had no choice but to collapse on his back on the kitchen floor. Seeing he was unarmed, Lisa had two more quick-fire thoughts; 'we're clear to move in' was the first, which she relayed to her partner with a simple hand gesture. 'What has he done with the knife?' was the second. A question that would come back around more than once over the next twenty-four hours.

They dragged the stricken suspect out of the flat as the rest of Lisa's team worked to dampen the fire in the living room and secure any evidence, having already declared the rest of the flat clear on their sweep. Paramedics were already on standby. They took over once Lisa was happy that the suspect was unarmed and was securely handcuffed to the stretcher that the paramedics brought with them.

The bullet from Lisa's standard issue Glock 19 had done more than enough to spoil any plans Rafik had of causing trouble soon. It had destroyed the femoral artery in his left leg, making it a real task for the paramedics to stem the flow of blood and save his life. Luckily, paramedics (especially those responding to calls on Moss Side) were bloody good at their work. They certainly had enough practice. Despite that, it took a lot of effort and more than a few blood transfusions at Salford Royal hospital to keep Rafik alive.

After it had been secured, the flat was inspected by Lisa's team. They found the twenty empty fertilizer bags in the main bedroom, which was untouched by the fire itself but badly smoke damaged, like the rest of the flat. There were no explosives to be found in the room, but they did find the intended use of the nails.

On the far side of the long room was a half-finished false wall. Timber batons were nailed in place across the width of the room, plasterboard was up across half of them, with more sheets yet to go on. Against the real wall, visible through the bare batons, were five shelves running the width of the room. Three of them, built one above the other, containing planters topped by hydroponic heating and feeding systems.

Lisa was horrified at what she saw. Rafik was just a weed-grower and, judging by the lack of anything that resembled a weapon, a harmless one at that.

Once he was stable in the hospital Lisa paid him a visit to interview him about his supposed involvement in acts of terrorism. The boy, he was no more than twenty-five years old, cried his way through the interview, pleading to be believed.

He said he had tried to run because he was sure the people breaking down his front door were the local gang, coming to take his supply. They'd been threatening him recently and he genuinely believed they were going to kill him if he didn't hand over his stash.

He didn't even want to grow the stuff, but jobs were hard to come by in 'Gunchester' and it was his only marketable talent. That was why he was building the wall, to protect his only means of making enough money to live, In the optimistic hope that he could pretend he'd quit growing when they came knocking again.

The sound that Lisa had identified as a knife being drawn was correct, but Rafik explained it was a normal butter knife that he was using to try to pry the top window open. It had jammed shut over time and he was trying to open it to get enough air to breathe.

Lisa knew after ten minutes with him that he was no more a terrorist than her own mother was. It was also clear to her that, had the paramedics not done such a great job of saving the lad, her career would have gone up in as much smoke as the stash of dried cannabis plants in the living room of the flat.

Within hours of leaving the hospital, Lisa established the 'tip' that took them to Rafik had come from a member of the gang that were known to run riot around the flats. It turned out they'd had a great night, watching events unfold from a flat on the other side of the green that ran between the blocks. They were handed over to the local police to be dealt with.

Lisa couldn't get past the fact that their intelligence hadn't picked up that the kid clearly was not a threat. How had they been so easily mis-lead by one scumbag making a phone call, and how on earth could they not differentiate between a harmless weed-grower and an active terror cell?

Lisa grudgingly acknowledged that was how things were, there was little point complaining about it. With limited budgets and resources, it was near impossible to be across everything. Sometimes you had to run with what you had, and that meant putting in the legwork on a hundred red-herring cases before finding one that was worth pursuing.

That was the feeling that she was getting again now. Standing in the security hub of the Trafford Centre with five other people. The two-man team working the consoles, coordinating with the guards out on the floors. Jason on the left and Imran on the right. The Centre Manager, Ben Hampton.

James Atkinson, Chief Constable of Greater Manchester Police, and her partner at SO15 of three years, Will Grant.

Will and Lisa were partners only in the work sense of the word. There had been one night, long ago, and before they were working directly together, where they had gone beyond the boundaries of a professional relationship, but that was a one-off thing the night after SO15 had put Lee Rigby's killers firmly away behind bars.

The tension of that day was more than anyone on the force had felt before. It made more than a few of them react in out of character ways. Some drank, some doubled down their efforts at work, others never recovered; losing their marriages and families as a result. Lisa and Will found comfort in each other that night after a few of them had gone for drinks to unwind. Afterwards, both agreed that it was simply a physical reaction to grief and stress and that they shouldn't mention it again.

Keeping that shared secret gave them a foundation of trust to build on when they were partnered together three years later. That trust had served them very well since. It was like they had a head start on other mixed-sex partnerships, having already gotten any tensions out of the way before they started, and they excelled as a team as a result.

Will often joked - when it was just them and nobody else could hear - that it should be a standard requirement that new partners sleep together before working together, to which Lisa usually gave him a sharp elbow in the ribs and told him to shut up.

Will thought she was embarrassed by the whole thing. He didn't know that she had feelings for him. She did a very good job of hiding that fact. She was far better at hiding things than Will was. The truth was, she hadn't been with anybody else since that night. Not because he was the world's greatest lover or anything, she just wasn't interested. She wasn't a one-night kind of girl, she needed a connection that was more than just physical.

Here now, she glanced at Will and could see that his eyes were starting to glaze over from the familiar routine of looking for something that just wasn't there. He had a habit of getting irritated quickly which got worse when they were sent on dead-end jobs. He'd already snapped off a few bitchy remarks to the two security guards at the consoles, when they slightly missed what he was directing them to focus on with the cameras. Unlike her, patience was not an attribute that Will could boast of. Fierce loyalty and ruthless determination were his strongest assets. Lisa valued those much more and so could easily forgive his outbursts of irritation now and then.

The guards working the console had no reason to value Will's attributes and it was clear that they could not forgive his remarks so easily. The responses from both had become curter by the minute. She couldn't help but notice the eye rolls coming from the guy on the right of the console whenever Will issued an instruction. He struck Lisa as a bit of an arsehole. Maybe he was one of those security guards that put on a front to deal with an inferiority complex. Probably, she thought. Most were.

Looking to take things down a notch Lisa said to Will, 'Why don't you go and see if you can grab us some lunch? I can handle this for a while.'

'Good idea, I could use a break from this bullshit and I barely had time for more than a quick bite this morning. Any preference?'

'You choose but make it something cold. It's already too hot in here without you bringing your bloody meat pies in here.'

'Salad it is then, spoilsport.'

'Salad won't do you any harm either Will, you could use a low-calorie meal once in a while.'

Will muttered something that sounded like "leaky ditch" under his breath as he put on his jacket. It took Lisa a second to decipher what he'd actually said, and she shot him a sharp look when she did, but let it melt to a friendly smirk when she remembered the already growing tension in the room.

With the door closed again, Lisa turned her attention back to the monitors. Privately betting with herself that Will would stop to scoff one of his precious Holland's pies before he got back with her salad. He was obsessed with the things, yet somehow managed to stay in pretty good shape himself. Lisa wasn't a fan of junk food. She thought that maintaining a good diet was half the battle when it came to staying in shape, although after a bad day she was partial to a bottle of red wine and a curry in front of some ridiculous TV crime shows. 'Elementary' was the recent binge. The number of episodes watched in one sitting would change, depending on how tough her day had been. There was something about the way that Jonny Lee Miller portrayed the modern-day Sherlock Holmes that soothed her soul. Plus, Lucy Liu always looked great. Lisa often stole fashion tips from her version of Watson.

Most of Lisa's colleagues were vehement in their hatred of TV police shows, but she found them therapeutic. She'd let the ridiculousness of them wash over her, carrying away the pain, malice, and inhumanity of what she saw on her worst days.

Lisa thought about asking one of the console jockeys to train a camera on Will to confirm her suspicions, but didn't want to lessen their already dimming opinion of her partner. She picked up her water bottle again and, after a moment of hesitation, reached for the briefing folder that sat alongside it. She figured it best to remind herself, for the fifth time that hour, what their target looked like. To keep the image fresh in her mind.

He *should* have been impossible to miss in a crowd. Aman Ali was a big guy, but it was his build more than his height that set him apart from the crowd. He was morbidly obese.

There was only one known photo of the guy. Taken over ten years ago, it was quite blurry but clearly showed him as a monster of a man. Will had commented when they'd first seen it that he should be easy to find because he was as wide as he was tall. He must have weighed at least four hundred pounds. He looked like one of those people you saw on TV complaining that half of their house had to be removed to get the crane in that would eventually get them out of their bed for the first time in fifteen years.

Lisa couldn't help but wonder how a guy of this size could possibly have gone under the radar for so long.

'At least, if he *is* here, we should have no problem catching him,' she'd said to Will as they walked down to the basement that housed the security office that morning. 'Even you'd have a chance at beating this guy in a running race Will. A slim chance mind.' she'd joked.

Digging Will out for being unfit or unhealthy was her 'go to' when it came to banter between the two of them. He'd never taken her up on her offers of joining her at the gym, preferring instead to go for a beer, and his love of junk food was famous in the unit. He'd always say that he was blessed with a good metabolism, and he certainly wasn't overweight by any means so maybe there was something in his claim. He carried a little timber sure, but that was a by-product of the drinking culture that he had always been around, first in the forces and now in the police service.

Lack of photos wasn't the only weakness in SO15's intelligence on Ali. They knew very little about him at all, other than he was believed to have links to the Brotherhood, the most dangerous breakaway faction of the recently defeated Islamic State, ISIS, ISIL, or Daesh, depending on which news station you followed.

Whatever name they were known by, they were finished in their known form and breakaway groups were now popping up all over the middle east. The 'Brotherhood' were the only ones that had popped up in Europe and they were being given serious attention at Counter Terrorism Command. Ali's link to them, if it was a link at all, was an opportunity for Lisa's team to gain valuable intelligence, and was enough to deem this a serious lead worth chasing.

Intelligence was sparse on the whole faction. The little they did know for sure, including the name Aman Ali and his supposed links to the group, had been gained by interrogating members of ISIS that were trying to bargain their way home to the UK, after it had become clear that there was going to be no Islamic State, and that staying in Syria guaranteed a death sentence.

How the hell these traitors had thought that appealing to the British public on the internet, saying that they'd made a mistake and were sorry, was enough to open the borders and let them back in was beyond Lisa's understanding.

Thankfully, despite the usual snowflakes flying the ridiculous human rights flag, those that called the shots had seemed to share her view of things, and vowed that no returning ISIS fighter would be allowed to return to a normal life.

They couldn't do anything else really. The rising nationalism in the UK, that led to Brexit even being a thing, was so strong on this subject that there would be riots in the streets if they had made any other decision.

Lisa was used to running on very little in the way of reliable intelligence, but the lack of it on this one scared her. It was standard practice now for terror groups to recruit and train insurgents specifically to blend into western society, before enacting whatever plans they had. What had Lisa worried now was that the Brotherhood, if everything was to be believed, were not your typical breakaway group.

What they'd learned from interrogation, and confirmed by working with Homeland Security in the states who had agreed to ask the same questions to their captives in Guantanamo Bay, was that the Brotherhood was far more than a breakaway group.

According to the Americans, they had been formed way before things fell apart in Syria. The intel suggested that this was a group of fundamentalists with a shared ideology that had been working together for a long time. They had been there and influenced the foundation of ISIS, having previously been involved with Al-Qaeda, the Taliban, and other groups over the years.

That was all they knew about the wider group. There were no pictures, no names, and no angles for them to use to find them. Except for this guy Ali.

If the intel was good, and Ali did have ties to the group, then maybe they could get a step closer to Hamza Al-Naswari, the leader of the group.

An "expert in insurgency tactics and recruitment of talent" the reports had said. He'd apparently gone through various personas over the years. Reinventing himself and changing allegiances as he needed to, when plans failed or money ran out, but every now and then he produced something that took the world by storm.

'Fuck me, we're looking for the Simon Cowell of international fundamentalism.' Will had joked.

Now they had a chance to do what nobody else had managed, to get a solid lead on Al-Naswari and maybe even lead the charge to capture him.

Somebody here, in her town, maybe even in this very building, had information that she could use to do that. Lisa didn't care how Aman Ali was linked to the Brotherhood. All she cared about was picking him up and getting what she needed from him.

The thought that he might be on one of the screens in front of her was like a waft of smelling salts to Lisa. Bringing her right back to the moment, doubling her determination to find the bastard.

It was a hell of a haystack to be searching though, even if it was the biggest needle in the world they were looking for. The security system had a footfall tracker in the top right-hand corner, a numeric display needed to comply with fire safety regulations, that showed the number of visitors to the centre today was nearly two-hundred-thousand already.

Hampton, the Centre Manager, explained that because it was bank-holiday they were expecting their highest traffic of the year today. Only likely to be outdone by the week leading up to Christmas. He had an air of arrogance when he explained this, like they were only coming here because of something he had done, and not for the shops themselves.

Whatever their reason for coming, coming they were, and in droves. Lisa could see all three of the main entrances to the centre on the screen, all of them getting busier by the minute. For every person that left the building, their business here done, another ten seemed to arrive.

She hadn't paid much attention to the ratio of overweight people in the building before, but now, looking at so many people in such concentration of numbers, she began to realise that this community was a perfect hiding place for Ali. Every third person on the screens was overweight.

Manchester was a metropolitan city. The same trends that were seen in London tended to spread to Manchester very quickly. It was overrun with fad eateries pushing the diet of the week; Paleo, Keto, Vegan, Gluten-free, Dairy-free, Carb-free. You name it, you could get it in Manchester city centre.

However, step outside the centre and head to the smaller towns and outposts of the area, *Greater* Manchester as it was labelled on maps, and it was a different story altogether. Chip shops and takeaways ruled the food scenes there. The area was famous for pies. It used to just be famous for making them, but now it was just as famous for how many the natives ate.

The fact that a good proportion of these pie-eaters had decided to make their way through the doors of this building this morning would make things a fair bit harder. She would have a job on her hands separating harmless fatty from possible fundamentalist.

As she watched the footfall counter continue to rise quickly, she felt a knot of nerves tighten in her tummy.

CHAPTER 5 – YOUNG ABDUL

Abdul had never been on a plane. He'd only seen them from the ground as they passed over, thousands of feet overhead.

Seeing one in person, walking up the steps to board the thing at Beirut international airport, had been scary and exciting all at once. He hadn't expected it to be so big, they looked so small when they were in the sky. When the huge bird took off, the sensation of his stomach lurching as the wheels left the ground made him think of how astronauts that he'd seen on the TV must have felt on take-off.

He shuffled his small eight-year-old frame, pinned back in his seat by the speed of the ascent, closer to his Mother. That's where he'd always felt the safest, and he was thankful that she was by his side now. As they climbed further into the sky, and his Mother enveloped him in her warm arms, he thought of his Father.

Why wasn't he with them? Why did they have to leave in such a rush without telling him where they were going?

Abdul was a clever boy. His Father was an accountant and his mother, who stayed home to raise him, was also a wise woman. They had taught him well to listen without speaking and to take in everything around him, even if he didn't understand it straightaway. When he'd heard his Mother talking on the phone to her Sister, just before they hurried out of their small home in the early hours of the morning, he had the feeling that something bad was happening.

He'd heard the word 'Hezbollah' through the guttural sound of his Mother's sobbing. He knew the word, but never understood what the 'Party of God' was. The name alone was exciting, without fully comprehending what it meant. He heard the same word a lot when he would pass the old men sat outside the market, as he ran errands and collected food for his mother.

Abdul always stopped and said hello to them whenever he passed. They were always nice to him; passing him bits of fruit or, on rare occasions, biscuits. Extra fuel to help him carry his grocery loads.

The real reason he always stopped was the radio they had. It was always tuned to a station that talked about football, and Abdul couldn't resist stopping to listen. He wasn't allowed a radio of his own and it was rare that he'd get to see any football on the television. They didn't own one and his Father's friends that did would rarely have it turned on when they went visiting.

Stopping and talking to the old men at the market was a treat for Abdul. Most of the conversations were football related, and Abdul loved witnessing the debates (arguments) that they would constantly descend into. Especially when the men included him, or asked him to settle a row on their behalf. He'd once been asked to give his thoughts on who was the better player: George Best or Pele. It was a no-brainer for Abdul. Pele was amazing but Georgie was a Red and that was enough for him. That particular settlement had earned him a couple of extra biscuits, making them even sweeter.

They didn't always talk about football. He'd heard conversations on all sorts of topics; economics, religion, and world politics being the other staples. He paid a lot less attention to those conversations, but he'd also heard them argue a few times about whether Hezbollah was a good or a bad thing.

Those were all subjects that he paid little attention to. He would zone out from their chat and tune in to the radio instead, but he didn't need to pay attention for things to stick in his memory.

That morning when he heard his Mother explaining that his Father was working for Hezbollah, he still didn't know what the word meant, but he now knew which side of the argument he would come down on if the men ever did ask his opinion; Hezbollah was nothing good.

They were going to stay with Abdul's Aunt in Manchester, England. His mother told him it was an eight-hour flight and they would have to stop on the way at a place called Larnaca in Cyprus to get more fuel. Abdul had never even left Beirut before today. He'd heard of Manchester. His Mother often talked about her sister and the life she had made there. It was also the home of Manchester United, his favourite team. In his mind it had always sounded like an exotic place, worlds away from his home in the Hamra neighbourhood.

Hamra wasn't a bad area, like others could be, but Beirut was small. No matter where you were, you could feel the ripples of trouble happening elsewhere in the city. Manchester, he knew, was a big city. His Mother often spoke about the second chance that moving there had given his Aunt, and how she was so lucky to be there instead of here. He would never say it out loud for fear of upsetting his parents, but he often prayed to go there one day. He was excited about finally getting to go, even if the circumstances of the trip, and getting on the plane without his Dad, were never a part of his prayers.

While they waited for their connecting flight at Larnaca airport, Abdul was told to wait on a seat while his mother went to call her sister again. Abdul always did what his parents told him and promised his mother he wouldn't move from where she left him. He had no intention of moving, the airport was quiet with not much going on when they got there and the seating was right in front of a bank of TV screens, one showing football highlights.

He had a natural talent for football, which allowed him to read the game very well for a kid of his age. When he'd played out on the streets of Hamra, while the other boys ran as a pack chasing the ball wherever it went on the pitch, he would be looking for the spaces where he could receive the ball and give his team the advantage.

His dream was to be a famous footballer one day. He loved hearing the stories of famous players like Rummenigge, Rossi, and Platini from the kind old men outside the market. Abdul would sometimes try to convince them that his favourite, Bryan Robson, was better than any of those others. He loved 'Robbo' and wanted to emulate him when he grew up. He secretly wished that one day those old men would be talking about him with such adoration. Maybe that why his mother wanted to take him to Manchester? He had always told her that he wanted to play for United when he was older.

Maybe there was nothing wrong after all? They could have been going so that Abdul could show them how good he was, and his Father would join them later?

As it turned out, the football highlights show was just finishing but Abdul didn't notice. He was too wrapped up in his daydreams. What would it be like to play in that great stadium? Would they cheer his name like they cheered for Gordon Strachan now? When he snapped out of his trance, he noticed that the TV had switched to a news channel, showing pictures of a strange looking building. To Abdul it looked as though they had stopped halfway through building it, leaving the entire front of the place unfinished, and then someone had set fire to it.

The news reporter, standing in front of the building, was explaining that the building was the U.S. Embassy in East Beirut. He explained that the death toll now stood at twenty-four, with another ninety thought to be seriously injured, although they were still clearing the debris and those numbers might well change.

Abdul wondered how something like that could happen. As if his question had been transmitted through the screen, directly to the man holding the big microphone and looking over his shoulder every few seconds, the reporter turned back to camera and answered him. He talked through a series of events that led up to the devastation behind him. Not much of the explanation meant anything to Abdul and he began to tune out again, until he heard the newscaster mention Hezbollah.

Abdul's blood temperature seemed to drop five degrees instantly, and he shivered as he listened to the report more intently now.

As the man on the screen continued explaining, it became clear to Abdul that Hezbollah was the name of a group of people that did things like this: setting off bombs and killing people for something called a Jihad. Another word that he knew the literal meaning of, but never fully comprehended what it represented. The meaning became clear then, and it became frighteningly obvious to Abdul that his father had somehow been involved in this horrible event.

His Mum was crying again, he saw as he looked over to the bank of telephones behind him, seeking the comfort only she could give. He knew then that he wouldn't see his Father again, that he was one of the twenty-four dead that the reporter had mentioned.

A sudden suffocating weight fell over Abdul. It trembled his bottom lip and made his limbs feel like lead against the chair.

His Father had always told him that he became the man of the house whenever his Father wasn't home, and that it was his job to protect his Mother. He tried to stop the tears from flowing with this thought, but it was too much to ask for a boy so young. His tears flowed thick and heavy, dripping from his chin into his lap, leaving a dark patch on the thigh of his trousers.

He turned to where his Mother was finishing her phone call and saw her wiping her face to hide the tears that she too had been shedding. Abdul did the same, using the cuff of his sleeve to soak the moisture from his cheeks. He didn't want to make his Mother cry anymore and, although he didn't fully understand what had happened, he knew that when he was upset it made her upset too.

The boy had always been intuitive, even at his young age. It wasn't something that he had control of, he just had a kind of natural empathy that meant he could pick up on the emotions of others. When his parents had argued in the past he would always know, even if he wasn't there when it happened. Perhaps it was in her tone, or her body language. Whatever it was, he always knew when his Mother was upset.

As she walked back to the bench that Abdul sat on, he knew that his she was upset now, but he saw something new too. A kind of strength in the way that she held herself that he'd never noticed when she'd been upset before.

As she sat down and wrapped her arms once more around her Son, he looked up to her face. 'Mother, did Hezbollah kill Father?' Her grip around him tightened sharply as she looked up at the TV screen he had been watching, and saw the news report that had triggered his question.

'Abdul, my beautiful precious boy. I am so sorry. Yes, your Father was killed in that horrible nightmare.'

'Did he do something bad Mother?'

'I don't know, my Son. The only thing that I know for certain right now is that it's not safe for us to stay here.'

A voice came over the PA system, announcing the British Airways flight to Manchester from gate 2 was now ready to board. Abdul's Mother said it was time for them to go. The boy wiped his eyes once more, nodded, and began to move, careful to stay by her side and keep a tight grip on her hand the whole way.

He spoke not another word until they landed in Manchester. He spent the entire trip in silence with his own thoughts. Thoughts of his Father's face, his Mother's fear, and the two old men outside the market were circling in his mind.

CHAPTER 6 – LISA

Why's he taking so long getting my bloody lunch? Lisa thought.

Now it was her turn to get impatient, and hungry, a mix that never went well. The younger officers around the unit called it being "hangry;" hungry and angry about it at the same time. A dangerous mix for anyone that happened to be in Lisa's vicinity when it kicked in.

She had earned a reputation over the years as someone that had to be fed regularly, or risk her wrath, and she was secretly proud of it. She kept herself in good shape - very good shape if the sneaky looks from the men in the control room were anything to go by - and didn't believe in denying herself pleasure, as long as she paid for it. She went to the gym regularly to pay that price.

She was aware of the power that keeping herself in shape gave her over a lot of the men she met. She found it hilarious that she could unsettle almost any man simply by playing with her hair as she spoke to them. How they became tongue tied if she leaned in close and spoke in a whisper. Silly things really, but powerful nonetheless, and invaluable as an asset in her work, tools that she used when she wanted something from people.

There were things about her body and her looks that she would improve if she could, and she was honest enough to acknowledge those in private, but they were not for others to know.

Outwardly she projected confidence in all aspects of herself, she understood that confidence equalled power. Lisa didn't believe in leaving anything unsaid, except for the most private of thoughts. If she was happy there'd be an obvious spring in her step and a smile on her face. If she was angry, those around her know this just as easily. No spring, no smile, but plenty of equally obvious signs, and often some collateral damage too.

It was a conscious choice for her to live her life this way, a choice that she'd made a few years earlier after learning some tough lessons about being a female police officer in a male dominated world. She had endured her share of the misogyny and sexism that seemed, for so long, to be the backbone of the police service, and this had driven her to make changes in how she portrayed herself, and what she was willing to tolerate.

Things had improved in recent years. A few high-profile and highly expensive lawsuits tended to have that effect, but nothing can change what's gone before and the memory of some of her old colleagues' behaviour still crept back into her thoughts every now and then. Instantly igniting her famously short fuse.

Lisa wasn't offended by being objectified or sexualised as a woman, she played on those things to get what she wanted, and she wasn't a snowflake, one of the 'Loose Women Lunatics' as she called them, that got on their soapbox, starting every sentence with 'As a woman...' and raving about equality and fairness in every aspect of life.

Her opinion, unpopular as it was with her female colleagues, was that all that did was swing the balance of sexism entirely the other way, punishing and marginalising men, and not solving the problem itself. She understood that it was therapeutic for some women to have that revenge, usually against some long absent arsehole from their past, but she preferred to get her revenge in her own, more personal and satisfying, ways.

She rarely shared these opinions outside of her closest circle any more. The backlash from her female colleagues in the past had been fierce, and they were entitled to their opinions too. Now, only Will in SO15 knew how she felt about it all. She couldn't help but let it slip during a tipsy debate about the 'Women in Policing' awards last year.

Will had tried to suck up to her by explaining what a "great idea" it was, and how it was "long past due." He dropped his pint, spilling it into his crotch when she punched him in the chest.

'What a load of bullshit!' She shouted. 'The whole idea of it is completely sexist and just marginalises both men and women. Just imagine Will, imagine the fuss that the Loose Women loonies would kick up if someone launched the 'Men in Policing' awards. There'd be hell to pay! Heads would roll, pensions would be stripped away, jobs lost. But, it's OK if it's just for women? If you can tell me how that's equality, I'll buy the drinks for the rest of the month.'

He had no answer to give and suggested they moved the conversation on, once he'd dried himself off of course. But he was going nowhere yet, Lisa was on a roll...'Equality, true equality, is simple Will,' she continued, 'nothing in the world should be about gender, *any* gender. Promotions, recognition, awards, *everything* should be judged by a person's ability and effort, and nothing more. Simple.'

Will agreed completely, but found himself getting uncomfortable anyway. He thought back to their active listening training session a few weeks earlier. He looked like an idiot, nodding his head constantly and throwing in verbal acknowledgements throughout Lisa's rant. He stayed quiet for a few seconds after she'd finished, to show that he was digesting what she'd said.

Lisa was quiet too. She didn't always like the response that the subject provoked in her, but she couldn't help it. She was vehement about her convictions on the subject, but she also knew that they came from a much darker place within her. The subject stirred up memories for her that were dangerous. They reminded her of feeling helpless; a feeling that she had always hated and that had driven her to the most extreme actions.

Her personal experience went beyond wolf-whistles and inappropriate comments. Hers were things done by people who thought they were untouchable, and the pain that she felt about them came not from the actions themselves, but from the fact that she was helpless. She wouldn't have been taken seriously if she'd complained about them.

She was not one of life's victims. She knew that she had to protect herself in her own ways instead, which meant being careful, being ruthless, and never being in a situation where it was just her word against someone else's. She became good at it.

Thinking about these things always woke the same memory in her. Back when she was still just a PC her old DCI, Jack Grayson - a real smarmy old pervert who was known as Greasy Grayson due to his long record of being inappropriate with new recruits - followed her into the women's toilets on a Thursday evening, after most other people had left the office for the day.

Lisa had been working late, trying to get ahead of the mounting paperwork on her desk that had been left to one side while she was testifying as a prosecution witness in court that week.

Grayson waited until Lisa was in the cubicle then walked quietly in, taking the cubicle next to hers and pulling the door to. He silently waited for her to leave her cubicle. When she did, he pounced. Grabbing her and dragging her in to the cubicle with him.

He was taller than her by at least a foot and had a good six-stone advantage over her in weight. Her build hadn't changed much since the age of seventeen; size 8 on good days, size 10 on the rest. In an unexpected tug of war, it was easy for him to drag her a few feet towards him and close the cubicle door again by throwing her against it.

What he didn't know, couldn't know until that moment, was that her petite frame was the perfect camouflage. Looking at her, nobody would expect the brutality that she was capable of when the right buttons were pressed.

Instinct kicked in as she bounced off the back of the flimsy cubicle door. She used the momentum to launch herself up at the panting, sweat-sheened, pig in front of her. She drew her fist close to her chest, making a sharp point with her elbow, swivelled her hips, and smashed her forearm into the bridge of his nose. She felt the bridge of his nose shatter against her arm and he stumbled backwards, falling to an awkward seated position on the toilet behind him as both feet went out from under him. He slumped, straight-legged with his toes pointing forward at a forty degree angle from the floor, looking like just another Saturday night drunk with no motor control. Confused, he raised both hands to his nose, a natural reaction to being struck unexpectedly. Lisa knew he'd do that instead of retaliating straight away. She also knew that she needed to put an end to this quickly before he got his bearings back, and more importantly that she had to cover her arse for the future, meaning just one thing. She had to take away his ability to put the blame on her. If she let him walk out of here, he could spin it any number of ways to make sure she was punished for not giving him what he wanted. But how could she stop him?

The answer came quickly, her synapses firing furiously thanks to the adrenaline surge crashing through her body, and it was as simple as it was effective; she just had to stop him walking out of there at all.

As the realisation of what had just happened began to paint a mask of rage on Grayson's flushed and heavily puffing face, Lisa twisted her hips slightly to the left, so that she her legs were almost side on to him, while her torso remained square. She planted her hands hard against the cubicle walls to her left and her right to take her weight and drew her knees up, lifting her feet off the floor so that her thighs ran parallel to the floor.

Grayson moved his hands from his face, the blood from his nose running freely down his wrists, staining his grey-white shirt, and lunged forward from the waist reaching for the front of Lisa's shirt, trying to pull her down towards him. His anger had clouded his vision. If he'd paid attention to what she was doing with her legs, he might've forgone the lunge in favour of sorting out his rag-doll legs and getting his feet back under him.

Lisa exploded her legs downwards with all her strength, and all her weight, landing both feet directly on top of Grayson's right foot which was helpfully still pointed at a forty-degree angle. All the weight of his leg was resting on his heel on the tiled floor and it gave her the perfect angle to land her blow. His ankle snapped instantly under her weight and power, causing him to slide forward off the toilet seat. Cracking the back of his head on the cistern as he did.

Damage done, Lisa wasted no time in getting out of there. Even before Grayson could get the first scream of pain out of his lungs she'd pivoted, shoving his head roughly out of her way and smashing his already broken nose off the side of the toilet bowl in the process, as she moved around the door and out of the cubicle.

She slipped out of the toilets and calmly walked away, out of the building. She didn't slow on hearing the screams of pain coming from the bathroom and she felt not a shred of remorse or guilt over what had just gone down.

Sure enough, the following day when she came into work, the office was buzzing with the rumours; Greasy Grayson had been caught short with a case of the runs, after a curry with the lads the night before, and decided to use the women's toilets, after having double checked there was nobody in there obviously. Somehow, he'd apparently managed to slip on the tiled floor, breaking his ankle and his nose as he fell.

There was no way that he could've said anything else. He couldn't walk out of that room - he couldn't walk at all - with those injuries, and so his only options, without implicating himself and admitting he'd been up to something in that bathroom, were either the bullshit story that he'd come up with, or to claim that he'd been dragged in to the room, by a woman a foot shorter and significantly lighter than him, and then savagely attacked for no reason.

Once his explanation was out, Lisa knew she was in the clear. He couldn't backtrack without proving himself a liar. She was pretty sure that Grayson wouldn't be bothering her again.

That was the last time that she'd had a violent run-in with someone at work, but Will was getting close to breaking that. How long did it take to get a bloody lunch?

It had to be a good 40 minutes since she'd sent him out of the ridiculously hot control room, and he knew better than to keep her waiting like this. Her water bottle had run dry and the temperature seemed to be rising faster than the footfall counter, which now read over two hundred and twenty thousand visitors for the day.

Lisa was determined to give the task her very best, but she was struggling to do that without at least a short break now.

When Will eventually backed into the room, carrying a subway salad in one hand and a Starbucks cupholder in the other, with two large cardboard coffee cups jostling for the upright position, Lisa wanted to either kick him for being so long or kiss him for thinking of getting coffee.

She wasn't sure which one would win, but the need for caffeine and relief she realised was greater even than the need for food, so she decided to let him off the kick, this time.

As he turned back the right way, sticking his bum out to stop the door from hitting him on the back, she saw crumbs on the front of his black T-shirt, the tell-tale sign that told her that she'd won her internal bet over the pie. That eased her mood significantly. The guy was predictable, which made him dependable.

'You look like a Kardashian with your arse stuck out like that.' she laughed.

'What the fuck is a Kardashian?' Will asked. His disdain for reality TV was almost as famous in their division as his love of junk food.

'Dude, do you seriously not know the Kardashians?' asked Jason, the security guard on the left of the console in disbelief.

'Must've missed it mate. I was fighting the IRA on the mean streets of Belfast when that whole Eastern Bloc thing was kicking off.' Will replied, making a mental note to look up where the fuck Kardashia was on the map when he got home.

Lisa nearly lost her bladder hearing Will trying to style out his lack of pop culture knowledge.

'About time, dipshit!' she said. 'I'm dying for the loo, coffee and food, and not necessarily in that order. It's your turn watching these screens while I go and take care of at least two of those things.' Lisa snatched one of the coffees out of the holder in Will's right hand, laughing as he struggled to adjust to the sudden shift of weight in his hand, and strolled towards the door.

The two guards on the console also shared a chuckle at Will's expense, earning the guy on the left a kick at the back of his swivel chair. Not hard enough to do any damage, just enough so he knew not to take the piss, and to keep his eyes on the monitors.

CHAPTER 7 – YOUNG ABDUL

Passport control in 1984 was a very different experience to what it is now. The queue was long. That has always been the case when coming into the UK. Since the late 1950's it's been a favourite destination for the world's displaced and disenchanted.

Terminal one of Manchester airport, one of the largest cities in the UK, was particularly busy. Being allowed access into the country was not a difficult task however, only a matter of time and waiting. A quick scan of a passport photo and a look over from the border agents and, providing they were happy, you were in.

As Abdul and his Mother passed the queues of people waiting in line at the baggage claim section (they had brought no cases, only the few items of clothing his Mother was carrying in her large handbag) Abdul's first impression of the place was how cold it was.

Outside the windows he could see the sky was a dull grey, like the colour of the smoke surrounding the U.S. embassy building he had seen on TV. The rain was pouring from the clouds, heavy and fast. Abdul had never seen so much rain. To him each drop looked as big as the hard lemon-flavoured sweets that he'd occasionally gotten from his Father, if he'd done a good job on his errands. He tried to count the raindrops as they waited at the doors of the terminal but quickly gave up. It was falling on all sides and as far as his eyes could see. He was surprised there were no rivers flowing in the roads. Instead there was a river of large black cars. Taxis, he surmised from the lighted signs on the front of each one, waiting with their engines running.

'Will we go in a taxi Mother?' asked Abdul. Another new experience for him if so.

'No Son. Your Aunt is meeting us here.'

Abdul couldn't remember what his Aunt looked like, but he had seen some old pictures and knew that her and his Mother looked similar. He scanned the faces around for someone that looked familiar.

Ten minutes passed as they stood shivering in the cold when he saw a young woman, pretty like his Mother, wearing a hijab and carrying a small red teddy-bear. Her face lit up when she caught him looking at her, and her footsteps quickened to a run. She bent and scooped him up, hugging him harder than he'd ever been hugged. She reached out and pulled her Sister into the embrace, and all three of them stood there for what felt to Abdul like an hour or more. His Mother's quiet sobs only just audible over the sound of the taxi engines and the noises of people happily coming and going through the terminal doors.

When they eventually released their grips on each other, Abdul noticed a huge man stood just behind his Aunt's shoulder. He seemed like a giant to the boy, towering above his Aunt's height, and almost four times her width. How had he not noticed the man before?

Abdul had once seen an eclipse back home. It was a strange thing, like the sun had been swallowed by the much bigger moon. Seeing this man stood behind his Aunt reminded him a bit of that, only the other way around. He was sun and he made his Aunt look insignificant in front of him. The boy had never seen someone so big, and fat.

It was his width that was the most startling thing about him. Abdul had never seen it, but he'd heard some of the kids at home talking about the movie Star Wars, and seeing this guy made him think of a character that they always mentioned call Jabba something or other. He was apparently a huge creature, built of pure fat, with no neck and no legs.

Looking now at this man, Abdul strained to see if he had a neck but couldn't see one. An immense black wiry beard hung down from his face, completely obscuring his neck, *if* he had one, and the collar of his robes. The size of his beard somehow made his head look tiny in comparison to the rest of his body.

Abdul's Father had been a small man. An Accountant by trade, he never had need for physicality and certainly he was nothing like the man in front of Abdul now.

His Aunt introduced her husband, Aman Ali, to them. His name, Abdul knew, meant security, shelter, or protection. How he could possibly offer any protection was a mystery. His bulk meant that he moved very slowly. His feet seemed to drag along the floor as he stepped forward, as if he couldn't lift the weight of his own legs. He leaned heavily on a cane for support as he moved slowly around his wife to speak to Abdul.

'I knew your father well Abdul. He and I were Brothers under Allah. I am sorry for your loss, but it is my honour now to help look after you, and teach you the things that he didn't get the chance to before he went to Allah's paradise.'

Abdul felt his mother's hand clench tightly on his shoulder as Aman spoke. 'Shall we go?' she said to her Sister. 'It's freezing cold out here, and we need to rest.'

CHAPTER 8 – HAMZA AL-NASWARI

As a boy Al-Naswari was one of those children that just couldn't stop moving. He was lithe and energetic and happy. Everything changed for him over time.

First in Syria where he grew up. His family was decimated over several short days in June of 1967, as Israeli planes indiscriminately dropped their powerful bombs on villages and towns in the region. That time became known as the Six Day War, a significant and important time in the history of the two countries. To him it was only known as the time that his life, before then peaceful and full of love, had changed completely. This was his first lesson in violence, and in rage.

That lesson became a constant one. As a young man in the foothills of the Afghan mountains, where he fled with his only Brother after his family had been killed, he endured daily the horror of hiding in caves and crevices as Russian soldiers seemed to come from every direction, constantly firing on them both without so much as a second glance.

They were still young then, barely able to fight back really, but they tried anyway. Throwing rocks and missiles and, whenever they found one, aiming the weapons they took from the dead hands of brave Mujahideen warriors to fire, badly, back at the Russians. Hamza's Brother Ahmed was killed by Russian bullets. Shot in the back as they tried to flee to safety. Hamza was on his own from that point on.

A young man of large build, he passed as much older than he was, and when he finally made it to Kandahar after days of walking alone and surviving on the last few rations that he and his brother had worked hard to preserve, he found a warm welcome in the arms of Al-Qaeda. Hamza found a purpose there avenging the atrocities that he'd spent his life witnessing.

With the funds being sent to Al-Qaeda by the CIA through Operation Cyclone, he got the training to support his purpose. Hamza stood out for his ability to think differently to others. His counsel was valued by the Al-Qaeda leadership and he quickly earned his keep as a tactician in the fight against the Russians.

He was instrumental in the development of insurgency warfare. Staying hidden in plain sight while infiltrating behind enemy lines. This was a skill that he'd had developed over years of running and hiding with his brother, and one that was used widely in the Caliphate that followed in later years.

After 9/11, which Hamza had no hand in planning directly, but was proud to know that his tactics were widely used, the relative safety he had found in Kandahar was safe no more. After the so called 'War on Terror' had brought widespread fighting to the region, Hamza was ordered to Lebanon to continue his good work there. The Al-Qaeda network was badly damaged by then and it seemed that time may be against him to strike the personal blow that he desperately yearned to.

He spent 2 years in Beirut continuing the work he'd started in Afghanistan, then moved on to Damascus in Syria, working with people that would later go on to set the foundations for what was known as the Islamic State. He trained them to recruit the right people, that could carry out their attacks in the most spectacular ways by going unnoticed in hostile territories.

After this Hamza decided that he had done enough for others. He grew tired of seeing others take the credit for his work. It was time for him to step out of the shadows and take his own action. He travelled under various aliases from Syria, through Europe, eventually landing in the UK.

He'd wanted to go to the USA but after the towers came down, the chances of getting into that Godless country were very slim. He settled on the UK as their closest ally.

Getting into the UK was easy. Despite being an island nation, their arrogance was such that they didn't even have a proper border in place. He paid a fisherman for passage on his boat into Scotland and made his way south across the hills to England, finally finding his way to the largest city in the Northwest, Manchester.

He'd been careful over the years to stay away from anything that would mean he could be noticed by others; no organised religion, he prayed alone and at home, only rare and careful contact with anyone that had ties with the old lands.

Aman Ali was his only method of contact with anyone.

Through Aman he recruited independently of the mosques and charities, that he thought were so obvious in their methods of seeking out disillusioned British youth to radicalise, and he stayed off the internet and telephones. He knew that intelligence services monitored all phones calls, texts, and internet activity. Besides, Hamza preferred to communicate directly and in person, ruling out any weak links in his chain as only he could.

It made for slower work for him to rebuild his Brotherhood in the UK, but he was secure in the knowledge that he had personally recruited all the Brothers and that nothing was left to chance.

CHAPTER 9 – AMAN ALI

Parked in the food hall of the Trafford Centre, surrounding by crowds of people, Aman reflected on the genius of using the mobility scooter.

He'd had it specially made to be bigger than standard scooters; wider and taller, so that his bulk would not stand out so much when he was sitting on it. Unless he was riding next to another scooter, the difference in his model was unnoticeable to the eye, but the effect it had on understating his size was amazing.

He couldn't hide his size completely of course, he weighed over four hundred pounds, but looking around at his current surroundings, overrun and bustling with people, he saw he was in similar company. There were at least another twenty mobility scooters parked within fifty feet of him, and very few people that could be considered slim. The communal tables that they were all sat at served every major fast-food chain in the building.

Despite Hamza's longstanding rule about avoiding mobile phones, Aman had one with him today. It was unavoidable given the size of the building they were targeting. Radios were out of the question, too easy to intercept, and it had been agreed as an acceptable risk this time. The time between Aman making the call to set the Brothers into action and someone at GCHQ interpreting what the call meant left no time for anyone to disrupt their plan.

It would all be over in a matter of minutes. The Brothers would be in God's paradise rejoicing their victory before the first infidel policeman set foot in the ruins of the shopping centre.

He pulled out his phone and dialled the number

CHAPTER 10 – THE BRIMSONS

It was only lunchtime and already the shopping bags were getting heavy. They'd barely been round half of the ground floor so far, having left some of Simon's hard-earned cash in the Superdry store, along with Foot Asylum, and Calvin Klein. Kids clothes were so blooming expensive nowadays, but it was Sophie's birthday so he could justify the cost.

'I'm going to take Soph' in here Simon,' Karen said, pointing at a shop that looked to Simon to be overrun with make-up stands. One of those places where you got assaulted by fake smiles and sprays of perfume from the second you walk in. 'Do you want to take Josh in to Game and check out the computer games while we're doing some girlie bits?' Karen and Sophie were more like sisters. They gossiped about everything, even boys, normally while watching Love Island together.

'That works for me,' said Simon. 'I don't fancy getting set upon by the painted lady brigade in there, and I certainly don't need to know any more about make-up than I already do.' Simon said as he winked at Josh. 'Come on Josh, let's go see if there's any new football games we can look at.'

Josh was the youngest. Aged just five. His cheeky little smile broadened as he realised he was getting some Daddy time. That meant he was bound to get a present too, even though it wasn't his birthday.

They had a busy day planned. Another hour or so of shopping, before hitting the food court for lunch. Josh wanted McDonald's but Sophie and Karen were both watching the calories and were pushing for Wagamama's. That battle would play out naturally Simon thought. After lunch, it was more shopping until about 3pm, then back to the hotel to get ready for the evening. Karen and Sophie were off to a concert in the City, a final birthday treat that Karen just couldn't resist organising for her bestie.

'What do you want to be when you grow up Josh?' Simon asked as they browsed the shelves of overpriced computer games in the Game store.

'Errr, a Footballer, but only on Saturdays. I'll be a wrestler maybe on Sundays, and then a policeman on Monday to Friday.'

'Do you know what mate? I think that sounds amazing. I think you can be anything that you want to be.' Simon meant it too. He often thought to himself how lucky he was to have kids who were so full of potential. Especially when the rest of the country seemed, to Simon, to be turning to shit with teenagers stabbing each other for no good reasons, or just knocking about on street corners, terrorising shop owners and locals for fun.

Sophie was maturing so quickly. Already halfway through her GCSEs and doing well so far, he thought. She was a level-headed kid with a passion for dance that made him burst with pride when he saw her teaching the younger kids at her school. Josh was as smart as a whip too. Always ready with an answer to anything, he reminded Simon of himself as a kid. He was enjoying watching the lad growing now that he was in school. Simon thought to himself, not for the first time, that he really could do anything in life. Simon tussled the boy's hair as they walked and said as much to him again.

'I know Dad, I'm good at everything. Now, can we find me a present before Mum and Sophie get back?'

Simon laughed. The boy knew his own mind, that was for certain. 'Sure thing mate, let's find you something. We need to be quick though, I promised Mummy we'd meet her back outside Kurt Geiger and I don't want to be late.'

CHAPTER 11 – ABDUL

Abdul folded down the phone and slipped it back into the pocket of his jacket.

He had his orders, and the time was drawing close. He felt his pulse quicken as he thought about what he was going to do. This must be what it's like to take drugs, he thought. It was like his senses were all heightened; thousands of different colours made up the crowds of people walking around him.

One stood out to him; a young boy in a full Liverpool kit, holding his Dad's hand and swinging a Game bag by his side wildly. The kid looked really proud of himself, a huge smile across his face as he shouted to someone ahead 'Soph, Soph, it's my birthday too, look!'

The sounds of the busy shopping centre fought to reach Abdul's eardrums first; people talking, laughing, he could even hear the clatter of plates and trays from the food-hall a hundred yards further in, towards the centre of the building, all ringing out to the backdrop of Rihanna singing about an umbrella.

The mention of rain took him back to that day outside Terminal 1. Still now, he'd never seen rain like that, but it was a passing thought as his mind moved quickly to his Mother. What would she think about what he was doing here? Would she be proud of him? Would she be horrified? Abdul would never know these things, and felt a sudden pang of anger at the bastard that'd taken her from him so cruelly.

Anger wasn't the emotion that would help him succeed today, so he squashed it back down to where it usually lived. Deep beneath the surface and hidden away. Not long now. In a few minutes he could finally let go of all that anger. All the pain that he'd lived with, since before his Mum died, going right back to that awful day that he was spirited out of Beirut.

Not for the first time, he wished he could go back to that day. To stop his Dad from leaving the house and to stay with them. They could've been so happy. They could've still come to Manchester, but maybe to live out his dream of playing football rather than...all *this*.

But dreams were as useful to Abdul in that moment as anger was, so he squashed that down into that same dark hole.

He'd let go of it all in one blast soon enough, and the whole world will see. The tiny Go-Pro camera that was mounted on his top, underneath his windbreaker, would take care of that.

CHAPTER 12 – WILL

Will perched on the edge of the desk at the back of the room, brushing the last few pie crumbs from the front of this top. He chuckled to himself, getting one over on Lisa wasn't easy, but he'd managed to get another sneaky pie past her eagle eyes. It was becoming a sport now, one that he was clearly better at than her.

He liked Lisa more than most of his previous partners but, pies aside, he couldn't get a thing past her most of the time. Little victories like this one had to be celebrated. His previous partners had mostly been rookies, fast tracked into the security services through sponsored university degree programmes. He didn't begrudge them that, it was how things worked nowadays, and it meant that he was normally the lead on any case they picked up, thanks to his experience in Anti-Terror Branch.

Will moved to the intelligence services in 1999. It was a tough transition for him to make. Until that point his life had been a military one. It was the family business, and as a boy he couldn't wait to follow in his family's footsteps when he was old enough. His Father had retired as a Regimental Sergeant Major in the SAS, and his Uncle was still a serving Captain in the Regiment when Will came of age to sign up. Their family was a close-knit unit, not unlike an army platoon, so it was a given that both Will and his cousin Luke would sign up when they could.

The family was based in Hereford, having moved when Will's Dad took an instructor role at SAS headquarters there. Will and Luke were both only children, both raised in and around Regiment barracks. Will was five years older than Luke, but despite this they were as close as if they'd been born Brothers themselves. Will took on the role of protector for Luke throughout their school years.

School in a military town could be a tough place. As well as the usual horrors of adolescence that all kids had to endure, there was another element that you didn't find in ordinary schools; wannabe soldiers that were being groomed to become warriors like their Fathers. Home was where they trained and learned the tools of that unique trade, but it was the school playground, and the alleyways, and playing fields around the town, anywhere that kids spent their time when not at home, that they put those tools to use.

Will had come to Luke's rescue more than once in their early years, but Luke was a true Grant boy. He learned to look after himself early, and by the age of eleven needed nobody to fight his battles for him. Will kept an eye on him anyway, it was his family duty. He understood what honour and duty meant and for a soldier, and a soldier-in-making, they meant everything.

Both boys fulfilled their duty of keeping the family tradition alive. Will joined up aged sixteen as a regular infantryman. His school grades were good enough that he could've waited until he was eighteen and signed up as an officer, but his Dad had always told him that to be a great officer you had to know what made a great soldier. That could only be learned in the mud and the trenches. Luke followed the same path when his time came, for the same reasons.

Will excelled. He was always going to. A legacy recruit with the upbringing that he had could rise through the ranks easily, if he kept his nose clean, which he did.

By the time Will was twenty-two he had served two tours in Iraq during the Gulf War, seeing heavy action each time, and returned home to successfully navigate the rigorous SAS selection process.

He served five years in the Regiment, four of them spent in and around Belfast. As far as the public knew, the SAS was never deployed in Ireland, but that simply was not true. The fearsome reputation attached to the Regiment, and the panic caused in paramilitary circles when it leaked that SAS boots, that were known to crush with much more force than ordinary grunt boots, were on the ground in Belfast was simply too powerful a weapon to leave at home.

Will enjoyed Belfast. It was just as dangerous as anywhere else he'd been posted, maybe more than some places, but there was something about a danger that was known and understood that, given enough time, made it comfortable.

After a six-month tour in Kuwait, Belfast felt like a holiday. Sure, it was an unfriendly place for an Englishman, but just the fact that he could understand what the people around him were saying was enough to make him more comfortable. Will was confident in any surrounding, he'd been trained for exactly that, but there was an extra level of danger involved when everyone around you spoke in tongues.

He could read the physical signs of danger well and he was able to pick up on atmospheric changes to situations that signalled trouble was coming; shifts in the proportion of men in a previously balanced crowd, or the way that voices suddenly hushed around him. These things signalled danger to a good soldier, and they were universal. It didn't matter where in the world he was; he could recognise them. What he didn't like about Iraq was that when these things *didn't* happen, unless it was an obvious physical danger he was facing, he had nothing to go on. He couldn't tell what was being said around him.

He might be stood right next to someone planning an attack, but if they did it with a smile on their face, and with no change in tone, he'd be none the wiser.

That wasn't the case in Belfast. There, if people saw him as the enemy, they had no problem telling him nice and clearly. "Fuck off you Fenian bastard" pretty much replaced "Good morning" as a greeting.

He still always had to be on high alert, ready for anything, but he liked Belfast. The divide between loyalist and separatist, catholic and protestant, was clear and that gave Will a black and white world in which to operate. That was a good thing.

In 1999, when it became clear that the Good Friday Agreement was going to hold and the peace process in Northern Ireland was succeeding, the black and white of Will's world began to merge back to grey again. That didn't sit well with him. He needed that clear definition of good versus evil, and it was this craving that pushed him to take up the job offer made to him by Special Branch in the last days of the Troubles.

Even now, Will preferred dealing with the Irish. They were a known quantity who had a set of rules that they stuck to. He admired that about them, and it made for a level playing field on all sides. Not to mention they were good enough to give warnings about the bombs they placed, meaning innocents could be saved in advance, instead of mourned afterwards.

He still couldn't get his head around how these Jihadis could twist the words of their own Quran to fit murderous ideals, claiming that their book told them to treat non-combatants with the same lethal methods as militarised governments, that they only ever seemed to aim their verbal assaults at.

At times it seemed to Will that it was all just a sick game that could never be won. Still, they insisted on playing anyway, to create as much chaos as possible, and disregarding any of their faith's rules that didn't suit their agenda as they did. It all came down to the same old human vices really didn't it? Money for some; there was a lot of money to be made through terrorism, just ask the guys that bet against United Airlines the day before 9/11. Others had different vices, all condemned by moderate Islamic faith; sex outside marriage, child molestation, drug trafficking and use.

It was funny, he thought, that the Quran rejected all these things and yet the ranks of those that fought the 'holy war' were filled with those that liked to partake of them.

Yes, he preferred going up against the Irish.

Most of all he liked the predictability, and blatant confidence of the IRA. Seven out of ten times when they were looking for someone in the IRA movement, they were found at their Ma's house, or their sister's house, or even sometimes their *own* house, sitting round having a cup of tea and having the belligerence to wear a "what the fuck do you want?" look on their faces when a British uniform banged at the door.

Not these Jihadis though, oh no. You had to be sneaky to find one of these bastards when they went underground.

Today's target had proven to be very hard to track down. Will knew this because he'd had Al-Naswari on his radar for a lot longer than Lisa and the rest of SO15 had.

His plan was solid. He'd worked on it for months in the hope that he'd get his chance, and now here it was. Putting it all into motion was the real reason that he had taken so long going to get their lunch.

CHAPTER 13 – YOUNG ABDUL

Abdul could barely contain his excitement as he hurriedly got ready for school. It was the first day of the new school year and his first ever day at Sutherland High School, the only secondary school in the Darnhill area of Heywood.

He'd been looking forward to this all summer long. He'd spent most of the holidays playing football with his friends on the fields, behind the garages at the back of his house on Crail place, practising to be ready for his move up to big school. He knew they had a proper football team that he could get into, even in the first year, and it was his first chance play in a real team, with kits, proper goals with nets, and eleven players in the team.

The closest he'd gotten at his last school was having a kickabout with his mates in the playground. Sometimes three against two, sometimes as many as four-a-side, depending on who else was playing out. Those days were fun, but they were not enough for him.

When he wasn't playing, he enjoyed coming and sitting on the banks of the fields on Saturday and Sunday mornings, watching the local teams play. They weren't as good as his beloved Manchester United obviously, but it was a long way across the city to get to watch them play and it cost money that he just didn't have, so he made do with watching the local teams, and imagining he was in the Stretford End watching his team play.

He always sat as high up on the bank as he could, to give him the feeling of looking down on the pitch that he'd experienced on the rare times he'd managed to go to Old Trafford. His Mother had saved as much as she could from her job, cleaning at the Highlander pub up the road. She didn't earn a lot and most of it went on paying the bills and feeding them both. She wanted desperately to be able to send him to a United game but just couldn't do it. He knew it wasn't her fault, but that didn't stop his disappointment when his school friends came in talking about the match.

His Mother died earlier that year, on a Wednesday while he was at school. She had been out shopping with her Sister, a day out for his Mother's birthday, when a drunk driver ran a red light and killed them both. His Uncle Aman was at the school gates to pick him up that day, and he knew instantly that something was wrong. His Mum never missed a school pick up, and Aman certainly wouldn't voluntarily walk to pick him up. Abdul had never known him to walk that far.

His Mum loved to quiz him about what he'd learned on the walk home across the fields, and Abdul loved being quizzed. He especially loved the days where he could amaze her with something that he'd learned. Usually it was something from a science or history class. She knew very little about those things and it gave Abdul a sense of pride to be able to share what he'd discovered with her.

The painfully slow walk home with Aman that day, stopping every fifty yards so he could catch his breath as his weak legs struggled to carry the immense weight of his torso, was very different. Every day since that one had been very different.

He didn't mind living with his Uncle, after all he'd been the closest thing to a Father Abdul had since he moved to England. The only problem really was that Aman had very strong feelings about certain things, like having a telephone in the house, or a TV. Things that Abdul's family never had back home in Beirut, and that he had enjoyed having since they had lived here.

Aman made them move after the two women died. He refused to live in that house, saying that it wasn't a proper Muslim home. Abdul learned what that meant when they got into their new house. Filling the space where a TV should go were prayer mats and a lectern holding a huge copy of the Quran. Abdul still had his own bedroom, which he was extremely grateful for, he'd panicked at first as he thought he might have to share a bed with Aman. One false move and he'd be crushed in his sleep! It was a naïve thought, but it scared him, nonetheless.

Abdul spent a lot of time in his room. Only really coming out at prayer and mealtimes. That suited him just fine. He sneaked copies of yesterday's newspapers into his room inside his school bag each day, courtesy of his favourite girl in school, who was his best friend outside of school too, Emily.

She would bring them in for him each day. She told him that her Dad always read the papers each night after work, and it was her job to put them in the bin after he'd done with them. She'd taken pity on Abdul after his Mum died, and started to put them aside for him after he'd told her about his love for football, and how Aman's strict parenting style was preventing him from staying in touch with it.

He would head up to his room after tea each day, when Aman's friends would come to the house for prayer group. They were a small group of men, all younger than Aman himself, and it was always the same men. In fact, the only time he could remember it being different was about a month ago, when one of the men just stopped coming. Otherwise it was always the same men, and always at the same times. Sometimes they'd be carrying briefcases, which Abdul thought was to protect their own versions of the Quran, and sometimes they would have big duffel bags with them. He didn't know what they were for and didn't really care.

He was only interested in going up to his room and reading his contraband newspapers. He'd read the sports pages all the way through, often twice. Soaking up all the knowledge that the writers shared about tactics, playing styles, and anything else football related he could find. Abdul developed a way to visualise the commentary as a live game in his mind, which had to be good enough.

He was thinking about all that he'd learned about the beautiful game as he left the house to head to school that first morning. He was going to show all of it to whichever teacher ran the football team, the first chance he got. First though, he had to call for Emily so they could walk to school together.

This was a new thing that they hadn't done before and he was excited about that too, only *slightly* less than the football. Sutherland High was in the opposite direction to his house than the primary school had been, and Abdul now had to walk past Emily's house to get to the new school, so they'd arranged he would knock on for her on the way.

Emily's Dad answered the door. Abdul had heard a lot about him but had never met him properly. Emily had told him that her Dad was the best, that he was super hilarious, and the most fun in the world, but she had never told him that her Dad was a policeman!

Abdul looked up at him in his uniform as he pulled the door open widely. He was a little scared at first, Aman had told him not to trust any policemen, that they were all Godless non-believers, but when the man smiled down at him and said "hello", Abdul didn't feel at all scared.

Emily came running out then, ducking under her Dad's outstretched arm and grabbing Abdul's, almost pulling him over as she shot past him. 'Bye Daddy. Love you.' she shouted over her shoulder without looking, and they began their journey into the new world of high school together.

It was a short walk from Emily's house to the school, maybe two hundred yards all told, but even so it felt daunting to the two of them. It would have been much worse if they weren't together. They both enjoyed spending time with each other. A lot. They walked the last fifty yards to the gates shyly holding hands. Holding fingertips really. They were barely touching, but they were touching, and it made Abdul feel like the luckiest kid in the world. That's when Abdul got his first taste of racism.

Unlike at the primary school, there were no teachers in the playground at big school. The kids were free to tear around until the bell went, so there was nobody to tell the gang of five boys hanging outside the school gates, smoking, to break it up or go to class. As Abdul and Emily walked past them, Abdul felt something hit his back. It didn't hurt at first, his backpack protecting him from the brunt of it, but as he turned to see what had happened the second stone hit him on the temple above his left eye. That one *did* hurt, it hurt like hell, and it sent him to the ground in a heap with a nasty cut above his eye. Emily went down after him, 'Abdul, what's wrong?'

'I don't know but it hurts' he said, taking his hand off his eye and seeing the red liquid on his fingers.

'Ha ha, should've ducked Paki.' Shouted one of the boys, which brought a round of laughter from the group around him.

Another chimed in, 'Find yourself a nice brown girl to walk to school with from now on.' The boys went back to the business of intimidating smaller kids as they went past, for any reason they could think of, not just their skin colour, while Emily helped Abdul up to his feet. They made their way quickly inside the school doors.

The two were in separate classes for the whole of the first day, something they were not expecting before getting there. When the bell went for the end of the day, they left through doors in completely different areas of the school. They hadn't planned for walking home. They both assumed they'd be in the same rooms all day, so they hadn't agreed on somewhere to meet. Abdul thought it best to head to the gates and see if he could find her. He got there first and saw the same group of boys hanging around by the gates.

With no teachers around again, he wrestled with himself over what to do. What if they started again? What if he waited for Emily and they threw more stones and hit her? He didn't want that to happen, so decided to head out of the gates by himself, quickly.

They didn't pay any attention to him this time. A ginger-haired Irish boy that had been in Abdul's English class earlier that day was getting all their focus, so Abdul slipped quietly out of the side gate. He felt bad for the boy but was grateful he had a clear run home and made the most of it. At a jogging pace, he made it home in four minutes, almost half the time it had taken in the morning.

Abdul felt a sense of relief when he shut the front door behind him. Once it was shut, he also felt a sadness come over him that he hadn't expected. He'd been so excited about going to school this morning. He checked if Aman was home and happy that he wasn't, he couldn't hear the usual laboured breathing coming from the living room, Abdul sat on the bottom stair and let the tears that he'd been holding back all day, maybe even since his Mother died, flow freely down his cheeks.

Fast, gentle knocking on the front door broke him out of his crying spell. He wiped his eyes frantically and looked through the frosted glass to see who it might be. He recognised the blonde hair and pigtails immediately and opened the door to Emily. 'Emily you can't be here, my Uncle won't be happy if he finds you here.'

'I know, but I had to see that you were OK. I waited for you at the gate, but you didn't come out. I was worried about you.' She said, the worry clearly visible on her usually upbeat face.

'I didn't want those stupid boys to throw things at us again, so I sneaked out while they weren't looking. I'm sorry.' Abdul said, feeling ashamed of himself.

'It's alright, I just wanted to see you were OK, and to give you this,' Emily shuffled her backpack off her shoulders and fished her arm inside, coming out with a whole copy of yesterday's Sun newspaper. 'I didn't have time to take out just the sports pages, but you can just throw away the rest.'

'Thank you.' Abdul said, his heart lifting slightly at her thoughtfulness.

'That's OK,' she replied, 'I'd better run, I don't want to get you in trouble with your Uncle, besides my Dad will be worried sick if I'm late home. See you tomorrow?'

'Yes sure, but maybe we should go in the gates separately tomorrow?'

'Maybe, but we can still walk together right? And hold hands?' Emily's smile as she added the last question was like seeing the sun shine through a break in the clouds to Abdul.

'I'd like that.' Said Abdul with a smile of his own, the first genuine one since crossing through the school gates that morning. He said goodbye to Emily and closed the door. With something else to look forward to, he ran upstairs to look through the paper.

Abdul threw the paper onto his bed while he shrugged off his own backpack and stowed it in his wardrobe. When he turned back to his bed, he saw the paper had fallen open on page eight, where he saw the headline "Paddington explosion linked to Rushdie Muslim Fatwa." Underneath the headline was a picture of a torn building front, with smoke still drifting upwards from the blown-out window frame.

The picture caught Abdul's eye, transporting him back to his seat in Larnaca airport and the news programme that was covering the U.S. Embassy attack. Instantly he forgot about the sports pages and read on.

Not much of it made sense. He didn't know what an "Ayatollah" or a "Fatwa" were, and he'd never heard of this man "Salman Rushdie". He wanted to read more so that he would understand, but before he could he recognised a name further down the page. It was a name he'd heard before, the name of the man that had stopped coming to his Uncle's Quran studies group a month before; Mustafa Mahmoud Mazeh.

He recognised the man's name because he had introduced himself to Abdul one evening, when the boy had let them in to the house. He remembered because he'd told Abdul that he too was Lebanese and had known his Father.

Abdul forgot about the sports pages that night. He forgot about the bullies at the school gates too. All he could manage to think about was the images of the U.S. Embassy, the pictures from the Paddington hotel, and that his Uncle Aman seemed to know people involved in both things.

He thought about asking his Uncle about it, and then thought about his Mother. What would she tell him to do? She and Uncle Aman did not see eye to eye on a lot of things, in fact they argued a lot when they didn't think he could hear them, but he always had. Not clearly enough to make out the words, but he could hear through the floorboards that their voices were raised, and not in a good way. He thought about this and thought that his Mother would tell him to say nothing, to stay quiet. She wouldn't want Uncle Aman to raise his voice to Abdul.

When he heard the unmistakable sound of heavy panting and slow shuffling of heavy feet, that signalled his Uncle coming in the front door, he decided to take his Mother's ungiven advice. He stashed the newspaper in his backpack, being careful to fold it back to the front page, and headed downstairs for tea.

CHAPTER 14 – YOUNG ABDUL

Losing a parent at a young age changes a child. Lots of kids grow up without their Dads around, it was practically a rite of passage at Suthie High, where Abdul was now settled into the routine of studying hard and avoiding any situation that might make him stand out from the crowds. Not academically of course, Aman insisted that he be at or near the top of every class he took.

To have a parent die was not the same as having one simply leave. There was no camaraderie to be had with other kids in the same boat, no replacement to be found in the shape of Mum's latest boyfriend.

Most kids never knew the pain and grief of outliving their Mum or Dad whilst still in school. In most cases kids became adults, even parents themselves, long before they ever had to deal with that kind of anguish. For the unfortunate few that knew the pain of having the roots of their family tree cruelly ripped from the ground underneath them, life became something different.

The dreams of the lives that they wished for, that they believed in absolutely while obliviously wrapped in the carefree cocoon of a complete family, lost their magic almost overnight.

What was the point of dreaming of happiness when you knew it wouldn't come? How could you ever be happy with such a gaping hole in your world?

Abdul knew it was pointless. He was a teenager now and had known that feeling since the age of six. It would always be with him, never to dull any more than it already had. Occasionally, immersed in the comforting print of the latest match reports, making smudge marks on his fingers as he traced the words and imagined watching it live, he let himself privately dream of footballing glory, but deep down there had been no real energy or belief in that dream since he came to England.

The loss of his Mother had triggered a new feeling in Abdul. Loneliness. Like other kids he had thought loneliness just meant being alone. He quite liked being alone, especially if he had an unread newspaper in his bag or if the grown-ups were arguing downstairs.

He knew now that it wasn't until someone spent time in the darkest corners of their own soul, that they would come to realise that you can be alone without being lonely, or that you can be surrounded by a million people, all holding hands, and feel isolated.

Loneliness was not what he was expecting it to be and the feeling of utter solitude, of not feeling like there was anyone to talk to, or that was interested in him talking, was hard for Abdul to understand.

Aman was there of course, but he'd changed too since Abdul's Mother had died. He became even stricter with Abdul, constantly citing verses from the Quran and telling Abdul how he was 'shaming Allah' if he didn't do whatever he was told. Clean the house, make the dinner, go to the shops.

Aman wasn't going to do any of it. He never had. He probably couldn't, the size of him. Abdul felt like the Cinderella that Emily had talked about so much when they were younger. Only instead of the wicked Stepmother and ugly Stepsisters that Emily had told him about, he was serving an obese distant Uncle, and a prayer group of very serious men.

Aman had insisted that in return for letting the boy move in and looking after him, the boy would join the prayer group and learn the teachings of Allah. Friday nights weren't what Abdul would consider fun, sitting around the living room. or serving tea to the others, all the time listening to them talking about the glory of Islam and how the 'infidels' of the west were desecrating Muslim lands. Having fun wasn't high on his list of things to do any more, and in a strange way it was nice to be surrounded by people that were at least familiar, if not familial.

At least it was interesting if nothing else. It had been getting more interesting lately too. He'd always been able to pick up on the moods of others and he'd noticed that things were changing in the group.

There was a feeling of tension building each week. He first noticed it when the men from the group, one by one, stopped talking to him when he let them in to the house. Then he'd noticed that they were generally talking less in the meetings too. Lately it'd been Aman doing *all* the talking, the others just listened in serious silence. Then, a month ago, Aman had begun insisting that Abdul go up to his room after an hour so the men could talk about 'other' things.

Abdul normally heard everything through the thin walls and floors of the cheaply built house, but not on those nights. It intrigued him what they were talking about and he desperately wanted to be included. Not that he would say as much to his Uncle, for fear of shaming Allah further.

Tonight, he had been sent to his room as normal, where he sat as quietly as he could, straining to hear anything that would give him a clue about what was happening downstairs that was so important.

Nothing was new in that respect, he'd been doing this for weeks now, but this day *was* different. Mainly because today was the anniversary of the day his Mother had died. While that didn't change anything about his grief, anniversaries mean very little to kids, it did make the loneliness worse. So much worse that he physically couldn't cope with sitting quietly and isolated in his room tonight.

He crept downstairs. Holding the handrail, stretching his right foot out and down to take him over the second stair, that he knew could be heard from the living room when someone stood on it. He managed to make it down the rest of the stairs in silence, the thin carpet cushioning his bare feet on every step.

With his ear not quite touching the door - he wasn't sure whether that would make a noise and didn't want to risk it - he held his breath and listened. Even so close, he couldn't make out any clear words. They must have been practically whispering in each other's ears. Frustration quickly overtook him, making him forget his grief for a moment, a blessed moment of relief, and forget any fear he might normally have had of being caught snooping.

Abdul glanced to the right where he spotted the men's coats hanging on the coat rack, on the wall behind the front door. Without any consideration of the possible consequences, he moved quietly across the floor and began riffling through the pockets of the coats, eager to find something, anything, that would tell him what his Uncle wouldn't.

What he found in the inside pocket of the third coat didn't give him any answers, only more questions. He was moving quickly, having not found anything in the first two coats, so when he snatched the folded piece of card from the coat pocket and unfolded it close to his chest, it took him a few seconds to recognise the faces of his Mother and Aunt looking back at him.

Confused, and conscious of the risk of being caught, he hurried back up the stairs as quietly as he could, being careful not to give himself away on the noisy stair near the top. Lying in the safety of his bed, Abdul held the photo in his hands tightly, as if the more he gripped it the more he could somehow hold on to them.

He was so overwhelmed to see their faces again, grateful that he could, he fell asleep that night still gripping the photo tightly underneath his pillow.

It wasn't until the next morning, on his way to school, that he questioned why it was that they were standing outside the police station in the photo. As far as he knew they'd never been in any trouble, he certainly hadn't, yet they were clearly just leaving the station when the photo was taken.

Maybe it wasn't what it seemed. There were others in the photo too. Maybe it was just a coincidence. Either way, he wasn't going to say anything to Aman about it. He had a picture of his Mum and he was keeping it, no matter what.

CHAPTER 15 – AMAN ALI

He needed to get in to position, and quickly, but his scooter was slower than its normal counterparts due to the excess weight it had to carry. He was heavier than the typical scooter rider of course, but that was not the main difference. The plus-sized were the main market for mobility companies, these things were built to be resilient. That's why he'd chosen it as his vehicle of choice today, but it was the modifications he'd had done that slowed the thing down more than anything else.

It wasn't possible to change the battery housing to accommodate a more powerful one and maintain speed, without compromising some of the dimensions he'd wanted, and he didn't think it mattered anyway. The attack was planned for a very busy day, so he wouldn't have been able to move fast through the crowds, no matter how powerful the motor.

Aman navigated his way down the disabled access ramp, toward the doors at the back of the hall, amazed that the architects had the forethought to make sure that even the disabled could move around freely in this place. It wouldn't have been the case in Beirut. There, people like him; the crippled, the infirm, and those with scooters packed full of explosives, would've never been able to do this. He chuckled to himself as he reached the ground level of the room.

Within the oversized fibreglass casing of his scooter were fifty pounds of steel ball bearings, wrapped around a core of highly explosive nitro-glycerine. It had been the hardest part of his plan to get this thing built. He'd known what he wanted from the outset but finding someone that could do it and keep their mouth shut about it afterwards had to be very carefully done.

Hakim had done a good job on the build. He was a good mechanic, that much Aman had known before bringing him in to do the work. The Muslim community was a close one, and in this area if you asked for a recommendation on a mechanic, there was only one name that was mentioned. He also knew that Hakim was a good Muslim; he'd watched him for several weeks before making contact and knew that he never missed prayers, closing his garage to accommodate things as needed, and he seemed to be devout in his faith. The real question was: Could he be trusted?

Allah provided the answer when Aman happened by the garage in late June 2017. It was the day after Darren Osborne had driven a van in to a group of faithful brothers, outside the Finsbury Park Mosque in London. Aman chose his timing purposely, so it would not be out of place for him to stop and strike up conversation.

'Brother Hakim, have you seen the news today?'

'Brother Aman, peace be upon you.' Hakim knew of Aman too, thanks to some of Aman's friends who had helped introduce the pair; Aman had collected one of them from their routine MOT drop off recently, and accompanied another to get his car serviced, both at Hakim's garage. 'I have indeed seen the news, and more than that, my phone has not stopped ringing all morning. The Imam at my mosque wants us to come out and protest at this mistreatment of our brothers this weekend. Tell me, is your mosque doing something similar?"?'

'I haven't heard of such plans. Actually, I wonder if it would do any good anyway'

'Funny, I was thinking the same thing. My brothers and I were the first to walk the streets in solidarity after the attack on the Manchester Arena recently. Even that same night as they were pulling people out of the building, we helped where we could and did all that we could to show that this was not an attack by all Muslims, but by only a few, and that we should not be retaliated against or contributing to making things worse. That was a big risk for us to take. We could have been made to regret our selflessness on that evening, but still we did it. But what was the point? Still our brothers in London have been mown down as they were waiting to pray. Of all places, on the doorsteps of Allah's house'

'I see what you are saying' said Aman, 'I've heard of other attacks on mosques more locally too. Not to the same scale, thanks be to Allah, but still it does seem that things are becoming more hostile towards those of us with peace in our hearts'

Hakim finished wiping his hands on an oil-stained rag and placed it down on his workbench. 'Yes, it does Brother Aman and, if I may confide in you, I'm not sure how much more of it I can stand'

Aman knew then that he could turn Hakim in to an ally for the Brotherhood. He'd seen the signs many times over the years; the self-doubt, the questioning, and frustration at the futility of a peaceful Islam, and he knew that he could persuade Hakim to help him in his mission.

Aman headed straight to the local car auctions from the garage that day and picked up a 1982 Jaguar XJS that needed a lot of work doing to it. It was in a very bad way, with extensive bodywork repairs needed as well as an entirely new engine. Because of the work needed, very few bidders were interested, and he managed to get it for just over £300 including commission. He had it delivered to Hakim's garage and became a regular visitor after that, having commissioned Hakim to work on the car, around his other work of course, no need to rush on this one. Aman used this excuse to visit weekly, to check on progress, and to share a cup of tea and continue the conversation that they'd started together.

After six months of regular visits, Hakim had agreed to help Aman with his project. He hadn't known at first what the intention was, only that he needed modifications making to a scooter. It was a surprise then to Aman when Hakim was the one that broached the subject.

'Brother Aman, I'm almost done with your project now, but before I put the finishing touches to it, let us sit and talk honestly for a moment'

'Of course, Hakim,' said Aman, suddenly worried that he'd misjudged Hakim's state of mind, 'what is on your mind?'

Hakim sighed heavily before continuing, 'I am a good Muslim, but I can no longer stand by and watch my brothers be persecuted as we have been discussing for months now. I am also not stupid. I know that you are involved in something, and that this scooter is part of that plan. There are many other models out there that are purpose built for, erm, bigger riders,' Hakim was clearly nervous referencing the giant's size, but something in him emboldened him to continue, 'the plans you gave me for this project are not just about reinforcing and making this machine bigger, they also create lots of space internally to hide something in. Tell me Brother, what is it?'

Aman took a few seconds before replying, watching Hakim for every one of them, looking for any sign of panic or fear that would signal to Aman that he was compromised. He saw none. 'Brother Hakim, you are indeed a good Muslim, and far from stupid. Before I say anything, can you assure me that this stays between us?'

'Between us and Allah, and if I break this vow may Allah's vengeance be visited upon me' replied Hakim, not nervous at all now, but confident.

Aman responded by lowering his voice to a whisper, deferring to the confidence of Hakim, a strategy he knew would work well to draw him in further. 'Then yes, I am on a mission set forth by Hamza Al-Naswari himself and I need the extra space to pack in explosive materials. As much as possible. It's a big open area that this will need to affect.'

Hakim smiled now, 'I thought as much. I know of Brother Al-Naswari of course, and if I may, I'd like to suggest something'

'Please do' Aman was genuinely intrigued now.

'Rather than packing this space with lots of explosives, which are no doubt hard to come by, I would use less and fill the rest of the space with these.' Hakim walked to the shelving rack behind him and produced a cellophane bag containing fifty 6mm hardened steel ball bearings. 'I think you might be able to get as many as four hundred of these into the cavity in the machine casing, and I could even replace a few more parts on the scooter with lighter alternatives to account for the extra weight of them. When the blast goes off, these things will fly in all directions and cause much more damage than just an explosion alone. What do you think?'

'I think it's a brilliant idea. Do it.' Privately Aman was disappointed that he hadn't thought of it himself. This was a basic thing that they'd used countless times in the old lands. His disappointment was short lived though as it dawned on him that Hakim had implicated himself in the planning by making this suggestion, and so he could not now go back on his vow.

Aman thought back to that exchange with pleasure now, sipping his tea in the food hall of the Trafford Centre. He took out his phone and opened the browser. He navigated to the website that he'd had built ready for today. Everything was running perfectly. He could see the streams from the cameras that he'd insisted the Brothers wear. Most were still covered under their jackets and coats, but he could see the shifts in light as they were moving around on the screen in front of him.

Soon those jackets would be removed, and the world would see his plan come to life. Aman looked up and around the great space full of restaurants and fast food counters. Each one at least five people deep in the queue, and every table in the hall taken with families sitting down to eat together.

There must be more than 3,000 people in here he thought, and not one of them will finish their lunch.

CHAPTER 16 – WILL

SO15 was created in 2006 when Special Branch merged with the Anti-Terrorism branch of the Metropolitan police. This combination of the two biggest anti-terror organisations in the UK had created one of the world's foremost units for proactively handling threats to the country. Not without cost though. Digitalisation of records was still ongoing when the changes came, and a lot of files were lost in the transitioning, including personnel records.

One of the files lost was an appendage to Will's own personnel record. Dated August 2003, the report detailed the death of Captain Luke Grant of the Royal Military Police, in Kandahar, Afghanistan. Luke had been killed instantly, while two others in his unit had been badly injured, when the vehicle they were travelling in struck a roadside IED.

Not much more had gone into the report, and not much more had been told to Will when he'd first been informed by his Uncle. It had been up to Will to find out more for himself.

He waited a couple of months to let things settle down then took a week of leave from Special Branch. He was determined to find out what had happened to Luke, and who was responsible. It wasn't hard to track down the two men that had been in the truck with Luke, Special Branch had the highest level of security clearance in the UK.

After they'd been rotated home from the base hospital in Afghanistan, he'd traced them back to their homes in the UK. Both had been medically retired after the explosion and were on civvy street now. He decided to give one of them, Neil Green, a visit. He was the closest geographically, just down the M6 in Stoke. Neil had been lucky. He had no permanent external injuries from the blast.

'I ride motorbikes Will' Neil explained after inviting Will in to his small flat above a kebab shop on the High Street. As soon as he knew that Will was Luke's cousin any paranoia or doubt about unknown visitors disappeared instantly. He was more than welcome. 'The injuries I got were like those I've had when I've come off my bike in the past. They bloody hurt, and really make you think twice about getting back on the bike again, but in the end you just *have* to get back on, it's too big a pull not to.'

'So why did you have to leave the service?'

'Bloody heart. My legs and back healed OK in time, but I've got something called "Atrial flutter" now. Means I've had to have a few operations to regulate my heartbeat and have to take a decent cocktail of drugs to keep it in check now. I wouldn't mind, but it means I've had to give up all the good stuff. No more smoking, caffeine, even alcohol, although that one is harder to stop so I just limit it. Don't tell my doc!'

'I'm not here to check up on your routine Neil. I want to know what happened that day.'

'Can't say I'm surprised. Luke talked about you a lot. Said you were more like his big brother than his cousin. He really looked up to you, you know? Anyway, he talked about you so much, I figured I'd probably hear from you at some point,' Neil opened the fridge and took two ice cold bottles of beer from inside the door. Twisted the caps off both, handed one to Will and took a long gulp from his own. 'I don't know what more I can tell you really. I don't remember much about the actual explosion. I passed out and didn't come around for a while, so I'm told anyway.' Neil took another, longer gulp of his beer, draining two thirds of the bottle in one mouthful. 'I swear to you, I'd have done anything to save Luke if I could, he was a good mate.'

Will nodded and pulled on his own beer before replying, 'I know you would. I don't blame you at all. It's the bastard that put the IED there I'm interested in.'

'Well that's easy. We were on a single-track road, headed to a house in the middle of nowhere. It was hardly a main arterial or anything, so there was no reason to think that there'd be any devices there. I'd never heard of them being anywhere other than major entry roads. We were looking for a guy that had been identified as a possible collaborator with Al-Qaeda, a guy called Hamza Al-Naswari. As far as our intel went, there wasn't much on Al-Naswari at all. His name seemed to pop up here and there but never with anything concrete about what he did. From what I've picked up from the lads still out there, turns out he's a ghost. Disappeared after the explosion and hasn't been seen or heard of since.'

'Thanks Neil, that's good. I appreciate your help.'

'Not at all,' said Neil, 'Like I said, Luke was a good mate. If there's anything else you need, just phone me.'

Neil wrote down his number on a slip of paper and handed it to Will, who pocketed it, drained the last of his beer and got up to leave, promising to call soon and visit again.

Will told nobody about what he'd learned. His Dad and Uncle wouldn't approve. They were unified in their view that a soldier must accept that death is part of the job and that the way to honour a death in battle is to go on to win the war. Will agreed, but that didn't stop him also wanting vengeance for Luke. That was the war that he was going to go on and win.

Will was fiercely loyal and determined. Lisa had used those exact words more than once to describe him, and she was right. It was how he was raised. A point of pride for him. He knew that whether he had to bend, break, or set fire to the damned rules to get the right result for the people he loved, then that is exactly what he would do.

Hopefully, he could do it whilst also keeping Lisa in the dark, keeping his job, and possibly his freedom too, if that were even all possible. If not, then so be it. Either way, he would not let Luke's death go unpunished.

CHAPTER 17 – YOUNG ABDUL

Growing up in Heywood was not easy for a Lebanese boy, or anyone that wasn't white and British. For a place with the nickname Monkey Town, Abdul thought this was weirdly ironic, but time has a way of getting people used to things that just are.

He'd learned early not to put himself in situations where he could become a target. There weren't that many situations he could get into because he kept himself to himself. The only real times he was at risk were on the football pitch, where he was an easy target for some of the boys because of his skin colour, but he saw that as a positive, because it had taught him to be faster, stronger, and to always expect the kick.

He could ride a nasty tackle better than anyone and, at the age of eighteen, he had proven himself to be tough enough to handle it more than once on the pitch. He let his football do the talking and was the leading scorer in his Sunday league team with only a few more weeks left of the season. He'd only picked up one red card along the way too. Things sometimes got rough out there. Most of the time he could play around it, he was smart enough to anticipate when a bad tackle was coming, and fast enough to react in time and make sure that most malicious kicks and high elbows hit nothing but air. Except in the game against Radcliffe Rangers.

Based just 6 miles away, Radcliffe was just close enough to make the two teams proper rivals. Not in the same way as United and City with fans giving each other varying degrees of abuse, terrace chants, and the occasional back street meet up to decide which fans were hardest. No, as much as Abdul dreamed of those things, at his level there were no chants, no terraces, and certainly no fans.

Despite all that, rivalry was rivalry, and none was fiercer than the one between neighbouring towns. During this derby, there was one player who managed to do what others couldn't and pushed Abdul over the edge.

He was just another typical thug in a football shirt. A white lad, a little older than Abdul, maybe twenty, and clearly a show-off. You could hear him before he got on the pitch, shouting and ribbing everyone in sight. The minute he took his position on the pitch, Abdul knew it was going to be one of those games. He was their right-back, Abdul was a left-winger, they were directly going up against each other for the next ninety minutes. It started straight away, the stocky right-back clattered into the back of Abdul as he was waiting to receive the ball from a throw in, flooring him, and laughed as he trotted back to his position on the edge of the eighteen-yard box.

'You alright Abdul?' Asked Jason, Heywood's captain and the closest friend that Abdul had on the team.

'Yes, I'm fine. Just another prick that I'm going to have to deal with. I've got it, you just make sure that they don't get through our back four Jase.' Said Abdul as got back to his feet.

'Don't worry mate, these jokers aren't going to get a sniff of our nets.' Said Jason smiling and backpedalling to the centre of the pitch.

'Good lad.' Replied Abdul.

The game went on with the usual niggles, and shit refereeing that you'd expect from a Sunday league game. Abdul was sure that the ref was still pissed from the night before, either that or he was as blind as a few players, from both sides, had suggested he was at half time.

With the score at 0-0 and seventy-eight minutes gone, Heywood won a corner. Jason was the corner taker, and a pretty good one, he found his target six times out of ten in training, which at this standard was as good as it got. As Jason was carefully positioning the ball in the corner, Abdul took up his position on the penalty spot.

Gobshite, as Abdul had come to think of the Radcliffe right-back, was right there with him, between him and the goal, and staying close. Grabbing a handful of shirt now and then, pushing and shoving, jostling Abdul to keep him off balance.

As the ball came in, high and seeming to float into the area, Abdul braced, bent his legs ready to leap and, just as he was about to launch upwards to get his head on the ball, the lights went out. Everything went black for a second as Gobshite's elbow connected with venom against the bridge of Abdul's nose.

When Abdul's eyes opened a few couple seconds later, he was looking up at the grey clouds from the flat of his back and he saw Gobshite's face come into view.

'Should've ducked Paki.' He said, laughing through the slur.

Abdul's brain was swimming, not just from the knock to his head, that hurt badly, but from the sudden recognition that the dickhead that had put him down was the same guy that had first introduced him to proper racism as a kid. Abdul felt a familiarity about him when he first saw him, but put it down to the stereotype of having a shaved head and a big mouth. There were so many people that fit that description around here that the whole appearance tended to blur a lot of people in to one big group, that could easily be labelled "generic twat".

Abdul climbed to his feet, checked his nose for blood, and brushed the dirt off his backside. Predictably the ref hadn't seen anything and play continued, much to Jason's disappointment who, Abdul saw, was in the ref's face shouting "Where did you get your fucking badges ref? Did they come free in a box of fucking shreddies?"

That earned Jason a yellow card, the twelfth of his season (almost guaranteeing him the club prize for biggest liability) and brought a whole group of players from both sides over to surround the referee. Not Gobshite though. He obviously wasn't concerned about what had happened and had gone over to the goal to grab a drink. Abdul saw his chance and broke into a run as soon as he saw the lad that had stoned him at the school gates turn his back.

He had nineteen yards to run and didn't give it a second thought. He kicked off like an Olympic sprinter and gave it everything he had. Out of the blocks he managed a decent speed in his legs by the time he reached the guy stood at the post, still with his back to him. Abdul kept accelerating as he got closer, pointing himself at the space immediately to the left of the bastard. When he got to within two feet, he reached out his right hand, cupped it around the back of the guys neck and, as he continued running, launched the unsuspecting bully's head as hard as he could in to the goalpost.

The sound of his face hitting the post Abdul thought was the most satisfying he'd ever heard. It wasn't a metallic sound, as somewhere in his mind he'd expected it to be, more like a dull, heavy, thump. The kind of noise you'd hear if you dropped a watermelon from a second-floor window.

When he turned to look, the guy was lying on his back, he must have bounced back off that white metal pole like a dead weight, out cold in one fast hit. His nose looked like he'd just taken the best that Mike Tyson had to offer in one unopposed hit. Abdul felt a sense of justice, that he didn't realise until that moment he'd always wanted.

Typically, the ref *did* see that. The melee around him had dispersed just as Abdul hit top speed on his run in, he'd seen the whole thing. Abdul took his red card like a badge of honour, walking off the pitch to jeers and threats from the Radcliffe players, and cheers and claps from his own, instigated by Jason who had forgotten all about his own booking and was now in a full-on fit of laughter.

That earned Abdul a reputation of being able to look after himself in the league, and he found things a little easier from then on. Once he'd served his ban and was playing again that is. The only thing now that stood him out from the crowd was his girlfriend. There were very few Asian or Middle Eastern lads that had pretty, blonde girls cheering them on from the side-lines. He might have been the only one. He couldn't change that, and wouldn't. Emily was worth anything that anyone could throw his way and he knew he could deal with all of it.

They'd stayed close all the way through school, avoiding public displays of affection of course, and were now officially seeing each other. Things were getting serious too. So much so that Abdul had moved out of the home he shared with Uncle Aman. He couldn't stand having to hide Emily from his Uncle and wanted more than anything to be able to bring her home and cook for her. He'd become a pretty good cook since his Mother died, he'd had to, because Aman refused to do it. Abdul wanted to be able to share everything with Emily, being free to invite her round was a big part of that.

It was tough to manage. His job at the mill didn't pay much, but if he was careful then he could manage the rent and the bills. His Mother had taught him that these things came first, and you could be happy without many extravagances in life. Except on birthdays, they were special.

Come Emily's birthday, Abdul had been saving for months to be able to do something special for her. They rode the number 163 bus into Manchester that morning. Normally they only rode as far as Middleton and got off to do their big shop there. One time they'd gone to Blackley, to a friend's house party, but this was the first time they'd gone all the way to the City Centre.

Abdul was taking her shopping in the Arndale centre. Nothing overboard of course, he wasn't made of money, but he had enough to get her a few bits of clothes he thought.

They arrived in the city early, around 9am, planning to make a full day of it, and had managed to get Emily a nice new top for when they went to dinner that night, before their plans all went wrong that was.

Shortly before 10am, the PA system in the Arndale sprang to life, telling them that the centre was closing and that all shoppers had to leave immediately.

'What's going on Abby?' asked Emily.

"I don't know,' replied Abby, 'but let's get outside and then we'll see."

They tried to get out the nearest exit on Corporation Street but there were police all around telling them they had to go to the other side of the building, and to hurry.

'Abby, I'm scared.' Said Emily, gripping his arm tighter as they picked up the pace.

'Me too Emily, but let's just get out of here, quick. Run.'

They did. They ran all the way to the other end of the building and filed in with the crowds pushing their way out of the doors. Outside were more police, moving everyone back one hundred yards, then two hundred yards, further away from the building.

Nobody wanted to move back. What was it with people that made them want to see something that was clearly not good, from as close as possible? Abby wondered about this often, whenever he saw a car accident and the rubber-neckers that slowed down or even stopped to watch the carnage. The last thing he ever wanted to do was watch someone being hauled from a crashed car.

Right now, the last thing he wanted was to be close to this building. He grabbed hold of Emily's hand and pulled her in to the crowd of people craning and shoving to get a better view. As they pushed through the crowd, they cut through frantic conversations and managed to pick out certain words being repeated; "Bomb threat", "IRA", "Terrorist".

The crowd must have been thirty people deep, making it hard work pushing their way through to the back. By the time they reached clear air at the other side of the crowd, it was evident what was going on. Abby stopped and turned to Emily

'Only a fool would stand around hoping for fireworks when the box clearly says bomb. Let's get out of here.'

Emily nodded, 'You don't have to tell me twice. Let me phone my Dad and see what's our best way out of here.' Emily's Dad had insisted she carry a mobile phone, despite the huge price tag that they carried. Emily's phone was a Nokia 8110. It had cost her Dad the equivalent of a month's wage to buy for her, but he insisted it was money well spent.

Emily walked further from the crowd, sheltering in the doorway of Thompson's Chippy to try to reduce the noise and hear better, while she listened to the ringtone that signalled her Dad's matching Nokia phone was ringing.

'Em, thank god. Are you ok?' Eric Matthews said. He was aware they were going to the centre today and had been worrying about her.

'Yes Daddy, I'm fine. We're out of the centre OK. I'm just calling to see what the best way out of here is. All the roads look blocked, so I don't know where to go.' Emily's voice was wavering with fear.

Silence...

'Daddy, Dad, can you hear me?' The fear now becoming audibly stronger.

'Em, sorry darling, my signal is....'

More silence...

'My signal is awful. Can you hear me now?' Eric came back.

'Yes Daddy, just. The line is awful.'

The line *was* awful. He must've moved to a better spot as it cleared a little. It was only the odd word that was dropping now, but Emily could fill in the blanks easily enough.

'Yes, I know. It's......bad here, I'm in the......storey car park......a vehicle check. I.......want to come and see........OK but......trouble at work and........the promotion interview's coming......know what to do.'

'OK Dad, I'll be quick. What's the best way for us to go?'

'You'll have to walk......a while, all the......are closed. It doesn't really matter which.......you go for now. Just get away from...... The only......... that matters is you.......sure you.......use Corporation Street. It's.......safe to go that way. Do you understand baby?' The muddle of words was interspersed with static, but Emily could piece it together well enough.

'I understand Daddy, thank you. We'll go right now. See you later, and please be careful. I love you.' Emily hung up the phone and moved out of the corner she'd been sheltering in. She took Abby's hand and said 'Come on

Abby. My Dad says it's best to move away. He said Corporation Street is the safest way to go, it's this way.' She pulled his hand hard enough to jolt his shoulder, reminding him of the first day they'd walked to school together. The fond memory made him follow without question.

Emily took the lead, pulling Abby by the hand all the way. Quickly they skirted along the back of the growing crowd, towards the corner with Corporation Street. Once around the corner they could see that the road was blocked fifty yards in.

'This doesn't make sense Abby. My dad said it was safe to go this way. He said it's *only* safe to go this way. Why would they block it off?'

'I don't know. Let's go and ask the police at the barrier.' Suggested Abby.

They headed quickly to the barrier, passing people going the other way that had been turned back. When they get close enough to be noticed by the officers guarding the barrier, Emily called out, 'Hey, why can't we get through here? My Dad's a policeman and he said this is the best....'

Emily's sentence was cut off as the wind was knocked out of her. She was thrown backwards as the solitary truck, a few hundred yards further down the road, exploded in a ball of white light, and her hand slipped from Abby's.

CHAPTER 18 – THE BRIMSONS

The argument over where to get lunch reached the only natural conclusion it was ever going to; a split decision. Sophie and Karen were indignant at the idea of being made to eat McDonald's. They were well into holiday prep mode, with their annual jaunt to Turkey coming up in just a few short weeks, and there was no way they were going to jeopardise their summer bods just for a Big Mac, no matter how hard Josh fought them on it.

Josh on the other hand didn't know what a calorie was. What he did know was you didn't get a toy with Wagamama's noodles, and he wanted a toy. The fast food chain was promoting the latest Marvel film and all Josh's mates had been showing their Happy Meal toys off recently, Josh was the only one that hadn't got one.

Simon was health conscious and would've normally sided with the noodles with no second thought, but sod it, he thought, the girls are going out tonight and I'll be at the hotel with Josh by myself. Alright, I'll get a few beers in but why not treat myself now too.

'I'll take Josh to get a burger and we'll meet you back here. Whoever gets back first can grab a table because they're filling up fast. That way everyone's happy and we can get on. Ok?'

'Yeah, yeah, you just want a burger yourself,' said Karen. 'I know your game. You can't fool me.'

'Well yes, that too. I'll just run an extra mile when we get home to burn it off.' Simon replied. He'd often have a little jab at Karen about exercising more. He didn't believe in controlling weight gain by dieting alone. If you were going to do it then you should do it for health reasons, and not just to fit a smaller size of clothes. That meant exercising too. Karen didn't necessarily share that view. At least not fully. She tried to exercise but found it harder than he did, she was always so busy looking after the kids and the house. Besides, dieting was hard enough by itself, especially if you liked a drink at the weekend.

Karen thought about explaining that for the hundredth time in response to his jibe, but instead just tutted at him, laughed, and turned to take Sophie across the food court to get their healthy lunch.

'Come on then Josh, let's go get the biggest burgers we can find.' Simon said as he took Josh's hand and began threading their way through the packed tables to join the queue at McDonald's.

'And a Happy Meal Dad, don't forget that.' Said Josh with a skip in his step.

They should really have walked round the edge of the seating area, but it was very busy and the queues for most of the food shops were backing out into the seating area as it was. They'd have had to cut through five or six different lines just to join the one they wanted. So through they went.

A few tables ahead Simon saw a man in a mobility scooter sitting at a table alone. He stood out because of his size. Even in the scooter, Simon could see he was a huge guy. He was spilling over the sides of the scooter. Rolls of excess fat hanging down to the sides of the seat. Simon had to assume there was a seat under there, he couldn't see one. He was tall too. Easily six-foot-four, maybe more, if he could stand up.

That wasn't the thing that caught Simon's attention though, merely what first caught his eye. The man had no food in front of him. Who would navigate to the centre of this tangle of tables and chairs if they didn't need to sit at a table? Especially if they were the size of this chap. Of course, he could've been waiting for someone to bring him something, but the way he was looking all around the food hall, rather than just in one direction seemed strange to Simon.

He shook it off and walked past (squeezed past) the guy in the scooter, bringing his focus back on to navigating the path ahead, without crashing into someone eating their lunch. Karen had told him about this before. He loved a good conspiracy theory, especially relating to 9/11, but he did also have a habit of being paranoid. Especially around terrorism. He'd once called the police to report a suspicious person stashing something inside a bin at the train station. He'd made Karen stay with him while they continued watching the guy from the other side of the platform. When the police arrived, in numbers and heavily armed, they didn't mess around. They pounced on the man, throwing him to the ground and pinning him there with weapons drawn. Only to release him after about a minute. It had turned out that he was a cleaner at the station. It was his job to empty and replace the bins around the place which is exactly what he'd been doing when Simon called in his tip.

Embarrassed, the pair had slipped out of the station, grateful that Simon hadn't left his name when he called the police. Karen had never let him forget it though and it was her high-pitched laughter echoing in his brain now that snapped him out of his paranoia and brought him back to the hunt for lunch.

It took an age to get to the front of the queue for their Big Mac and Happy Meal, and Simon couldn't help but glance back to the big guy in the scooter. Still he was glancing around a lot and seemed to also be checking his phone and watch a lot too. Despite Karen's whining in his ear, he couldn't shake the feeling that something was wrong with this guy.

"See something. Say something." The slogan kept circling round in his mind as the last person in front of them in the queue finally got their order and moved aside. Simon looked across the hall to the Wagamama's queue and could see that Karen and Sophie still had a few people in front of them. That made up his mind for him. He could get their food, find a security guard, and get back to find a table before Karen even knew that he'd done it.

With any luck she would never know that he'd said anything to anyone. Unless of course he turned out to be right, in which case he'd make *sure* she knew! Either way, he wouldn't be able to enjoy the rest of his day unless he did something.

CHAPTER 19 – LISA

'This is fucking impossible. There are too many people in this place. How are we supposed to spot one guy in these crowds? Might as well be looking for a specific piece of hay in a field full of fucking hay-bails' Lisa was getting fed up now. She wore frustration on her lips like others wore hearts on their sleeves. Will often said that her language was like something he'd expect to hear on a Friday night in a Docker's bar.

Hampton, the Centre Manager, winced at hearing Lisa swearing so loudly. Clearly, he was a bit prudish when it came to language like this. Will liked it. Foul language was part and parcel of Army life and on the odd occasion he heard it now it felt like putting on a favourite pair of slippers. Warm and comfortable.

'Please, Officers. I need to ask you to keep the language to a minimum. *My* officers need to be able to communicate on the radios and tannoy. I can't have that kind of language being transmitted across my centre' said Hampton bullishly. He really was a cock and he was starting to get on Lisa's nerves. Emphasising *"My officers"* as if trying to exude authority over the room, making it clear that they were guests in *his* house.

Lisa turned her head sharply to glare at him. After a second, she raised her eyebrows, changing the meaning of her look from 'what did you say?' to 'if you've quite finished?' in an instant. No matter how he interpreted it, the manager got the message and got back in his box quickly. Physically shrinking backwards in the room and looking down at his phone as a way of breaking eye contact with Lisa.

Will caught Lisa's eye and struggled to contain a laugh as he saw her mutter something under her breath

'Twat.'

The exchange was enough to bring all their attention back to the screens on the wall and silence prevailed again. It was short lived, as one of the speakers embedded under the monitors on the right-hand side of the bank burst in to staticky life.

'Control from Gamma 3' a robotic sounding voice crackled through a speaker in the monitor bank.

'Go ahead Gamma 3' replied the guard on the right-hand side, Imran.

'Control, I've had a report of a suspicious person in the food hall. Any chance you can pan across and monitor?'

'No problem Gamma 3,' said Imran, 'what section am I looking for?'

'The guy who reported it said he was central. So should be section E or F. He's an IC4 male, riding a mobility scooter. Apparently, he's a big guy, six foot four at least, three hundred pounds, maybe more.'

'Ok. Wait one, Gamma 3' said Imran as he fiddled with the joystick that controlled the cameras.

'Don't worry, I've got it.' Said the guard on the left of the console, Jason, panning and zooming the cameras they needed much faster than Imran had managed. Will and Lisa were up on their feet now, leaning over the backs of the guards' chairs. Both had sprung to life hearing the description of this suspicious giant and were waiting anxiously for Jason to get the right camera in place.

'Here we go. This is the right angle, just need to zoom it in a bit,' Jason focused the lens in tight on the man in the scooter. It wasn't exactly an HD quality picture. The camera that he had to use was mounted on the ceiling of the food hall, they couldn't get a direct shot of the man's face.

'Is that him?' asked Jason.

'Christ, I don't know,' said Lisa. 'it *could* be. Is there not a better angle to use?'

Jason shook his head without looking in her direction. 'No. There is another camera that would be better, but it's obscured. See?' he said, pointing to another monitor in the top right of the bank.

'What's that in the way?'

'Balloons. They're forever being released in the food hall and get stuck in front of the cameras. It's a right pain in the backside.'

'Fucking *brilliant*!' Lisa erupted, swivelling to direct this tirade at Hampton. 'You're telling me that we've been in here for hours, sweating our tits off, putting up with your bullshit, looking for someone who can give us the first decent bit of fucking intel into a genuine threat to national security, and now that we've got a possible lead, we can't get a proper look at the prick because of some fucking balloons?'

Hampton was incensed, his face turning an instant red. 'What do you want *me* to do? Tell the restaurant chains that they can't give balloons out to kids? They'd laugh in my face.'

Lisa covered the six feet between her and Hampton in three quick strides and screamed in his face like Gordon Ramsay after being delivered a cold beef wellington 'No, of course not, God forbid! But at least keep your *fucking* cameras clear of obstructions. Is *that* too much to ask?'

The useless manager was visibly shaken by the verbal assault. He was known to dish out hairdryer treatments like this one, normally to cleaners who couldn't afford to answer him back, he wasn't used to being on the receiving end of it.

'I'll get maintenance down there now to clear them away,' he whimpered, loosening the collar of his shirt, trying to release the incredible heat he could feel on his face.

'Don't do us any fucking favours' Lisa said, more calmly this time, turning back to the monitors. She was sure he might piss himself if she carried on shouting and, as much as she was tempted to see that happen, she knew that would just make him even more useless than he'd already been.

'What do we do now?' asked Will.

Lisa tugged the sleeves of her jacket in turn to settle it back in place. 'I don't know. We can't move until we can confirm it's him. That place is packed with people and lifting someone that size isn't going to happen unnoticed. If we've got the wrong guy it could spook the right one, then we're screwed.'

'Won't the maintenance people do that anyway? If it *is* him it'll be pretty obvious seeing them going up a ladder to move a balloon from a camera pointed right at him.'

'No,' said Jason. 'they won't need to climb up. There is a mezzanine that runs behind the walls with access points behind the camera positions. They were put in especially for maintenance work. They won't be seen from below.'

'Ok good. How long will it take to get them cleared?' asked Lisa

'Ten minutes, fifteen at most' replied the guard.

'Jesus. Ok, do it. Will, what do you think?' she asked.

'I think it needs to be five, not fifteen. We can't wait that long for confirmation. I'll head up there in the meantime too, just in case.'

Lisa checked her watch. 'Ok that works. I'll stay here on the cameras and confirm once we have a clear view.'

Will turned on his heels and headed for the door. 'Great. Use the radio though, my mobile signal might not be great in some of these walkways and I don't want to miss you.'

'Agreed. And Will, be careful. Don't go in to that hall until I give you a GO.'

As the guard got on the radio to maintenance, Will headed out of the door and along the tunnel to the stairs. He pulled out his mobile and checked his signal. Five bars. Perfect signal. Just like last time he used it in this tunnel.

Will didn't need any more confirmation but was grateful for the extra time that moving those balloons would give him. He had known as soon as he saw the picture appear on screen that it was his target. He hit the button for the second speed dial number on his phone and bounded up the stairs two at a time while he waited for the call to connect.

'It's Will. We're on. Ali is here in the food court. He's disguised himself by riding an invalid scooter, that's why you haven't spotted him yet. He's in the centre section, parked at a table by himself. I'm on my way to you now, I'll be thirty seconds. It's time to take this bastard out.'

CHAPTER 20 – ABDUL

'Abby? Abby, is that you?'

Only one person ever called him that. Hearing the name again after all this time froze his blood and took the breath right out of his lungs. Not just because it could *only* be Emily's dad, but because Emily's dad was a police officer.

Abdul was panicking. What was he doing here? Why now? He hadn't seen him since the funeral and the guy just happened to turn up here, today, what were the chances?

He knew he had to turn around. To ignore him would rouse suspicion and he couldn't risk that now. Was he going to be alone? Did he have his handcuffs out, ready to take Abby in?

He swallowed, took a breath, and turned slowly around to face Eric Matthews.

He wasn't alone but he wasn't backed up by armed police either. On either side of him, holding his hands, were twin girls. They looked to be about eight years old. The same age Emily was when Abby first met her.

'How are you doing, Son?' asked Eric, 'Long time.'

Abdul relaxed a little. He clearly wasn't there on police business. He was just another shopper going about his day.

'I'm doing ok thanks Mr Matthews. It *has* been a long time. I'm sorry. I meant to come to the house after the funeral and everything, you know, to pay my respects. I just wasn't up to it. I'm sorry.'

Eric smiled bitterly at the mention of his daughter's funeral. 'Hey, don't worry about it. I'm just glad you're OK. I was worried about you for a long time. I came to the school to see if I could catch you there, but the teachers told me you were being home-schooled. I tried your old house, but I guess you moved too?'

'Yes, that's right. My Uncle thought we needed a fresh start, what with everything that happened, you know?'

'Yes, I know how that goes. It was hard for all of us. These two were my fresh start,' said Eric, 'this is Jenny, and this is Carrie,' he said lifting each girl's hand up in turn to show which was which. They really were identical Abby thought, 'aren't they just the image of our Emily?'

'Who? Emily? No, I don't see it' Abdul said, a little too quickly. He followed it up quickly too 'I'm sorry, that was insensitive. I must've spent too much time with my uncle.'

'That's ok. How is your Uncle? Aman wasn't it?'

'Yes, that's him. He's doing ok. Still the same.'

'Good. Listen Abby, do you have time for a coffee? There's something that I wanted to talk to you about. I was hoping to do it years ago but what with Emily I...' Eric's voice choked slightly at the mention of her name. '...I struggled to cope for a while. Things got lost in the fog of it all. But there is something that's been playing on my mind for a long time. Guilt in a way. I should've found you before now to say it. Give me half an hour. What do you say?'

The last thing that Abby wanted to do today was sit down, drink coffee, and talk about Emily. He didn't need to revisit the pain for a start. Today was about getting *rid* of the pain. He also didn't need coffee. His nerves were beginning to shred as it was.

'I'm sorry Mr Matthews, I'm just leaving. I've got to be at work soon. How about I pop round tomorrow and stop in for a coffee then instead?'

'Oh. Yes of course. Please. You remember the address?'

'I remember.'

'OK great. I'll see you then. I'm really pleased I bumped into you Abby. It's great to see you.' Eric leaned down to the girls and tousled their strawberry blonde hair 'Come on then girls, let's go get you those new ballet shoes. Say bye-bye to Abby.'

'Bye Abby' they said in unison.

'Goodbye.' Abdul replied. Knowing with absolute certainty that he'd never see any of them again.

He was relieved at that thought.

CHAPTER 21 – YOUNG ABDUL

How could she be gone? She was so vibrant. So full of life. For years Emily was the best part of Abdul's life. In many ways she was the *only* bright spot in his life. Now she, like his Mother and Father, was gone and there was nothing he could do about it.

He didn't know what to do with himself. He couldn't bring himself to get out of bed in the morning, never mind go to work or play football with the lads. After a week of not turning up, he didn't need to worry about work anymore. They replaced him easily enough. It was hardly rocket science work. The football lads were more persistent. They didn't expect him back straight away, but he found he didn't have the energy or the motivation to get up and play at all. After three months of holding his place open and trying to check in on him, even Jason gave up. Jason had called almost non-stop to check on him, even coming to the house a few times. Abdul never spoke to him, just asked Aman to make excuses for him, which he did willingly.

Aman was brilliant in those early days and weeks. He was like a completely different man. Movement was still slow, and he still broke a sweat just getting out of his seat, but in terms of how he interacted with Abdul, he was completely changed. It seemed to bring out a caring side of him that had been well hidden before. Abdul thought that it must be a shared grief thing. They'd both lost the woman they loved.

Aman didn't encourage him to get back on the horse or to go out and do something. He was happy for Abdul to cut himself off from the world for a while. Aman enabled it by making sure that there was plenty of food in and that anything Abdul might want was on hand. Even his newspapers in the early days, until Abdul shared that he'd lost interest.

Aman didn't go to the shops himself of course. He'd never have made it back, even just carrying a couple of pints of milk would be too strenuous for him. Aman called on his Friday night prayer group instead. They came around a lot more often in those days, looking in on Abdul, making sure he knew he had people there with him and Abdul was grateful to them for that.

Although the pain never went away, it did dull over time. Abdul came to rely on Aman and his friends. There was something soothing about being part of a group with shared beliefs.

He felt safe in their company. After a while, he could talk about his losses and the pain that they caused him. The group came to be like a family after a while, and Abdul found a lot of answers through them. In the early days he was full of questions. Why did his Mum have to be taken? Who was responsible? Why did Emily's Dad send them in the wrong direction on that fateful day? Why would Allah allow him to suffer so much in his lifetime?

After months of wrestling with these questions he came to see, with the help of his new family, that he was not being punished by Allah, but that it was the people of this town and country that had taken everything from him. The group helped Abby realise that the things that had happened to him, his family, and his beloved Emily, were not his fault. Nor were they accidents. They were the direct result of the society that he now lived in. One where family and faith were sacrificed in place of immorality and selfishness.

The group helped Abby to see that it was Allah's will that he should take his own retribution for their crimes.

CHAPTER 22 – AMAN ALI

He couldn't help but feel exposed. Sitting at the table in his oversize scooter, seeing how his presence there caused others to have to make extra efforts to get past him. He chastised himself for not having foreseen how this would make him stand out.

He was finding that it was a lot harder to keep track of all the little things when you were operational. He put it down to his advancing years and vowed to pay more attention. One step at a time. Allah willing, he would only need to keep his wits about him for a little longer.

The first step was to change the current situation and move to a new position that wouldn't compromise his cover. He reversed the scooter as far back as he could from the table, enough to turn a hundred and eighty degrees, and headed for the wheelchair access ramp. Once back on ground level Aman manoeuvred towards the doors at the back of the food hall. He reached the doors and positioned his scooter just to the side of them, facing inwards.

He thought again what a good job Hakim had done. There were close to 500 ball bearings inside the scooter casing, all the way around the frame, and not a single sound was made by them as he had weaved around the obstacles in his way.

Aman assessed his new position. He still had clear lines of sight to both major entryways into the food hall. His position by the rear doors was perfect. Scanning the expanse of the room he could see almost everything that he could before, except for the ground level on the opposite side of the room. The raised seating area, that he was previously positioned atop, for high ground advantage and a full three-sixty-degree view, was now an obstruction to his field of vision. A large one. He calculated that there was roughly one hundred square feet on both sides of the room that he now could not see fully. There was nothing of strategic value in those spaces, he still had full visibility of all the key points in the room including all the fire exits and maintenance doors.

The cameras were still obscured by the balloons that he'd had Abdul release on arrival that morning. That had been one of the more complicated details to make work, especially considering it was more of a precaution than a necessity. He had a much more effective way of staying ahead of security, but it was his nature to be thorough.

Aman had to observe the food hall for weeks to figure out the best way to eliminate that camera. Getting up there to disable it was not possible. Even posing as a maintenance crew they couldn't take the risk of drawing attention by using ladders. As far as he could see that was the only way to disable them fully.

It was on his fifth visit to the centre, three months earlier, that he saw the solution and realised that disabling the camera may not be the best outcome. After all, if it was out of action then surely there would need to be a repair made, and he could not control how quickly that might take place.

A group of children, aged between three and seven, had been crowded round a table singing happy birthday to another child, sat at the head of the table. A flustered young woman stood holding a birthday cake, with a burning candle in the shape of a number six, by his side and was singing with them.

At the end of the song, all the children stood up clapping and cheering. As they did, one of them knocked over their chair and the three helium filled balloons that had been loosely tied to the back of it had slipped free. Aman watched as they floated up from the chair, ribbons snaking gently behind them.

The balloons came to stop at the first obstruction they met. This just happened to be the bracket that held the security camera. Two of the three nestled underneath the camera housing while the third bounced around looking for somewhere to settle. After a few seconds it found its settling point, right in front of the camera lens.

Aman was amused by this. How something so innocuous could achieve what he'd been puzzling over for weeks. He waited to see if they stayed in place by themselves or if they would eventually float on as the gasses inside demanded. They might also be removed, by order of the people watching on the other end of the cameras. He settled in for a while longer to see which outcome it would be, making sure to refresh his cup of tea occasionally so as not to appear out of place.

The balloons had been loosed at midday. By 5pm they were still in situ in front of the camera. Aman had seen no sign of anyone coming to check on the obstruction, never mind remove them.

Five hours was more than enough for his needs. All he had to do now was establish where to release the balloons, which was easy enough. As he left the hall, he mentally marked the spot where the fallen chair was still lying.

There was the risk that, on the day, they may not come to stop in the right position, but it was an acceptable risk.

A high-pitched beep, the signal for a text message being received, snapped Aman back to the present. Who was texting him now? He'd made it clear to the Brotherhood that there was to be no contact of any kind. Unless there was a problem.

Aman scanned the room once more before reaching for his phone. He wanted to be sure that he was safe before giving his full attention to the message.

Satisfied that nothing was awry, he opened his phone and clicked into his inbox. What he found waiting for him there meant that he wasn't as safe as he had first thought. It also meant that he had a decision to make, and quickly. Go now, or abort?

He ran the options through. They had to go now. Too much planning had gone into this to walk away now, and the only thing that he was still waiting on was final positions being confirmed by the Brothers at the eastern doors. Even if they weren't quite there yet, they couldn't be far away and could improvise.

Aman tapped away on his phone, opening the draft email he'd saved. The 'To;' line had a string of addresses preloaded, ready for when he wanted to hit send; BBC news, ITV news, Sky news, as well as Al-Jazeera back home and Fox news, CNBC, and ABC in America. Sending to all was the best way to ensure that his message reached the whole world at once.

He hit send and navigated back to his text message folder. He reopened his last message, the one that had moved his schedule forward, hit reply on his phone, and typed out a return message, hitting send straight away.

Lastly, he opened his Whatsapp and selected the group chat that he'd set up for the martyrs that were here with him today. Three words, no more.

"Go. Allahu Akbar"

CHAPTER 23 – WILL

Will opened the locked maintenance door on to the concourse, thanks to the passkey that he'd been given by the security team when they'd arrived. That was about the only thing they'd been useful for. He knew that security guards were generally known for being lazy and incompetent, but even so the two that he'd spent the morning with so far were a cut above the standard. The centre manager too. Bad attitudes and bugger-all brains between them.

Now, up against the clock, he hoped that incompetence extended to the maintenance team too. He needed all the time he could get.

Walking fast, he couldn't run in case there was also a camera on him now, he cut right into the Starbucks a hundred yards to the right of the access door.

He found Neil sitting at the back of the shop, far from the view of the cameras out on the walkway. A large black holdall occupied the seat next to him and a smiling played at the corner of his mouth. Neil was putting away a prescription bottle after shaking two tablets out on to the table in front of him. As Will took the seat opposite, Neil popped both pills into his mouth and swallowed them down, without the aid of the lukewarm coffee sitting in front of him. Neil looked pumped, his eyes were bright, he looked more vital right now than Will had seen him look before.

The two had stayed in touch since that first meeting. Will had thanked Neil again by text after he'd gotten home from meeting him the first time. From there, the texts became quite regular. Their shared connection with Luke gave them a bond that quickly became a friendship. They were comfortable with each other, with similar experiences, as well as the link through Luke. Even down to language and sense of humour. People often mention that the friends they make in the forces, any of the forces, are the best they will ever have. What they don't often mention is that a shared sense of humour is one of the strongest foundations of that unbreakable connection. Spending months, years, with the same group of people has that effect, especially if that time is spent in combat.

They met up for drinks every week or two. Neil shared stories from his time on tour with Luke. Will shared stories from their youth and from his own work, both in Ireland and more recently too. Neil seemed to come alive when they were telling their stories. It was like he was living them again. Will supposed he was in a way. He couldn't imagine what it was like to be forced to retire from the service without anything to look forward to.

It occurred to Will that he and Neil were a lot more alike than he'd first thought. In the same situation, Will would miss the life too. More than he could imagine right then.

The two began meeting up every other Friday night for a few beers. Neither had many friends, another symptom of being a veteran, so it worked well for them both. It was on one of those Friday night meet ups that the seed, from which today's plan had grown, was planted. The two were playing pool, a favourite between them and a fierce competition. As it stood Will was in the lead for the month, having won twenty-three games to Neil's meagre eighteen, including a fantastic seven-ball clearance from the break, that he just would not let Neil forget. The running deal was that whoever won, over the course of the month, had a wings and ribs platter and a whole night of beers paid for by the loser at the start of the next month. Then the counter would reset and round they'd go again.

Will was confident of another win this month. Cocky even. Neil had pretty much conceded that he was going to have to cough up too, so neither was paying as much attention as normal to the game.

Out of the blue, Will looked up from the table and asked Neil 'if you knew where Al-Naswari was, what would you do?'

Neil grinned, 'That's easy my friend. Eye for an eye. If it's good enough for the bible, it's good enough for me.'

'Even though it'd mean prison?' asked Will.

'Do me a favour.' said Neil, standing up and spreading both arms out to the side. 'Have a look at my life mate. No missus, not even an occasional one. No service for me anymore. Christ, I can't even get a civvy job now with this broken ticker. What life?' He took a deep pull on his bottle of Peroni and raised his bottle towards Will by way of a toast. 'This poor excuse for a night out with you is pretty much the highlight of things for me, how fucking sad is that?' Neil laughed and lent back down to the table to line up his shot.

'I'm serious mate.' Will replied.

'So am I! You're asking me if I could get the chance to do what I'm good at again, *and* take that motherfucker out in the process? Abso-fucking-lutely I'd be on that. Just a shame nobody knows where the fucker is.'

'Don't they?'

Neil stopped cueing his shot. Putting both hands on the edge of the table, he looked at Will. For the first time all night, seriously.

'Will, do you know where he is?'

'I shouldn't say anything else mate. I'm sorry, I shouldn't have said this much. I've obviously had one too many.'

'No Will. You can't just leave that there and back away from it. This is Luke we're talking about. He was like a brother to me too. If you know where Al-Naswari is, you *need* to tell me. Look, I understand that you can't do anything, what with your job and all, but *I* fucking can and you know that arsehole deserves it.'

Will drained the last third of his pint in one go and grabbed his jacket from the stool next to the bar.

'Neil, mate, I know you loved Luke too, and I can't tell you how grateful I am to you for that. But I can't let you get involved in this. You're right, he does deserve payback, and I promise you he's going to get it, but it's going to come from me and nobody else' Will clapped Neil on the shoulder and squeezed, then turned and headed out the door of the pub.

Neil grabbed his jacket too. Leaving his beer unfinished, he ran out the door after Will, catching up to him in the car park just as Will was opening the door to his car.

Will knew he shouldn't be driving, but he knew his limits and he knew he was ok. Besides, if he *was* pulled over, he'd only have to flash his ID and raise his voice a bit and the copper would be too shit scared to do anything other than wave him on his way.

Neil grabbed the top of the door frame, stopping Will from closing it. 'Listen, Will. I get it, I really do. And I get that you're only trying to keep me out of bother, but mate, I'm not Luke. I know how you looked out for him, but you don't need to do that with me. I'm a big boy, I can handle myself. More importantly, I was in that truck with Luke when he died. I didn't get the chance to look out for him then, and that kills me.' Neil's voice broke slightly with that last sentence and Will saw his eyes had welled up. Neil took one hand off the doorframe to wipe at his eyes and took a second to compose himself. Will said nothing, knowing that there was more to come as soon as Neil could get it out.

'Al-Naswari didn't just kill Luke that day Will. He killed me too. He took my best mate away. He took the whole *army* away from me. I was gonna be a thirty-year man. Taking that away is the same as taking my life, I know you know that. Now look at me. I've nothing. Now there's a chance that I can get some payback for that. I can get some payback for Luke too. God knows I owe him that. You can't leave me out Will. You know I can help you.'

Neil wiped his eyes again, with both hands this time. Will didn't shut the car door. He was frozen looking at Neil's face. The dams of his eyelids had given way and his cheeks were shining with reflections of LED headlights, shining tracks of hot tears running down his face.

'Get in the car.' Will said after Neil dried his face.

Will explained that they were only going to speak when it was safe, and that did not include in the car. They drove the rest of the way to Will's flat in Cheadle in silence.

Once inside, Will pressed one finger to his lips to show Neil that it was not yet safe to speak. He headed into the bedroom and came back carrying a small black rectangle. It was about the size of a TV remote with just one button on the top of it. Will pressed the button and placed the box on the coffee table in the middle of the living room floor.

'Ok, we're good now. That's rule one. We don't speak about any of this until the jammer is turned on, understood?'

'Sir, yes Sir!' snapped Neil. 'So, what's the deal?'

Will reached under the coffee table and ripped free a black document file that had been taped underneath. 'A few days ago, we got intel that this guy' Will pointed to a picture that sat at the top of the open file, 'Aman Ali, has ties to a terrorist outfit that Al-Naswari is involved with.'

'What kind of ties? Does he know where the bastard is?' asked Neil urgently.

'Give me a minute! Aman Ali wasn't on any of our watchlists, we've never heard of him before, so it was slow going to begin with. I couldn't find anything on the guy, so I widened the net, and I found something in records today that got me thinking. While his name is clean, there was an old report on file from a Nayna Azim who used to live in the same area. It wasn't a full report, it hadn't been completed or submitted, but there was enough on there to make it worth a look.'

'Ok, so?' Neil had always been the impatient type.

'This woman Nayna went into her local nick with her sister, claiming to have information on Hamza Al-Naswari' explained Will, deliberately taking the pace slow so he could finish making the pieces fit in his own head.

'What information?'

'We don't know. But that's not the important thing here. Nayna Azim and her sister were both killed the next day in a hit and run in Heywood town centre. Her sister's name was Fatima. Fatima Ali. Her husband was Aman Ali'

'Ok, that's no coincidence. So, what do you think? Aman finds out his wife's sister has gone to the coppers, feeds it back, and Al-Naswari has them killed?'

'Something like that. Or Aman did it himself, but he's a big fat fucker and I don't really see him being the type. But at the very least he knows *something*. This is the first time I've had anything to go at on this, and I know I should let the unit deal with it, but there's no guarantees they'll get anywhere. Chances are he'll just lawyer up and go no comment once they pick him up, and the chance will be lost. I can't let that happen.'

'So, what's the plan?'

'We do it our way. If you want to help, the first thing we need is weapons. Untraceable weapons. Think you can handle that?' asked Will, the serious expression unmoving from his face. If there was a point where Neil would brick it and back out, this was it.

'Definitely. I've still got my own personal stash at home, but anything else I can get from the lads still in the unit.' Neil was backing out of nothing.

'Good,' Will said with more than little relief. He really had no idea how he might've pulled this off by himself and was grateful for Neil's support. 'We don't need loads. 2 MP5's and 2 Glocks, one of each for both of us, is more than enough. We're not going for all-out war here, it's only this guy that we're after.'

'Consider it done. When is it happening?'

'I don't know yet. We know this guy's name, but as far as I've seen, he's like a bloody ghost. That's good for now, gives us time to get the guns on standby. When I know more, you'll know. Then we just need to get to him first and grab him without being nabbed ourselves.'

That had been three months ago. Now, sitting in Starbucks, Will felt like it had been a lot longer since they had that conversation. Neil was true to his word though, as proven by the presence of the holdall next to him. Will reached over to the bag, hoisted it over the table and took it with him to the toilet. He locked the door behind him, opened the bag and took the Glock first, tucking it in to his waistband at the back of his jeans, below the longline T-shirt that he'd bought specifically to give him more coverage for this. Two extra magazines went into his left-hand jacket pocket and one extra mag for the MP5 into his right.

The MP5 was the perfect gun for what he needed today, short barrelled and compact, it tucked easily under his jacket and with a shoulder strap attached to the stock that hooked over his shoulder, he didn't have to try to hold it in place and make it obvious he was carrying something. With his jacket zipped back up nobody was any the wiser.

Neil had already loaded up with his own arsenal so Will folded the empty bag as many times as he could and, on his way back to the table, shoved it right down inside a bin.

Now armed and ready, Will leaned down close to Neil 'Thanks again for this mate. Now let's get it done.' He straightened up and header for the door.

'Absolutely. For Luke.' Said Neil, as much to himself as to Will.

Neil drained the last of his coffee as he watched Will leave. The idea was that he'd leave two minutes later, so that they were not seen together on the main cameras. They had to be careful. They were taking big risks, but both agreed that while there was a chance of getting vengeance for Luke, they had to stay the course.

Will had just grabbed the door handle when a thunderclap shook the door, and the huge glass panes that made up the front walls of the shop, exploded inwards in a blizzard of shards and splinters.

Will was thrown to the floor by the force of the blast. The reinforced door that he was holding had taken the brunt of the shockwave, and held strong, thanks to the additional wire reinforcement running through the glass panes within. Patrons of the shop that were, until a second ago, sat by the windows enjoying their complicated coffees and herbal teas, were thrown askew all over the shop, peppered with flying glass. From his prone position, Will could see injuries ranging from minor cuts, on the older woman in the far corner, to what he was sure was a fatal jugular wound on a young barista that had been clearing empty tables.

Will had only moments to register what had happened, before more huge blasts rang out from other parts of the building.

CHAPTER 24 – LISA

'Where are these fucking maintenance men?' Lisa asked, over her shoulder, for the third time in the last five minutes. Her eyes hadn't shifted from the screen showing her possible target.

'They're on their way. They were on a job on the other side of the building, so it's taking a bit of time to get there.' Said Hampton, more subdued and compliant after having been on the receiving end of Lisa's acerbic tongue.

'A bit of time? I could've gone and done this myself by now' she replied sarcastically.

'You're very welcome to try.' muttered Hampton, the impulse to play the alpha in the room slipping his control, and earning him another sharp look, this time from Chief Atkinson.

'If you could refrain from commenting please Sir. This is a delicate situation and we're all stressed, but I can assure you that none of us wants to be here and the soonest we can be out of your hair we will be.' Atkinson stood full height, from the perch he'd been occupying on the edge of a desk, and took a step towards Hampton. The action reminded Lisa of a Westlife key change back in the 90's. There was nothing musical about the move from Atkinson's perspective, he was asserting his height advantage and subtly, much more subtly than Lisa could ever manage, using his body language to intimidate the little man. 'That said, none of us are leaving until our business here is concluded. So, in simple terms, the sooner you shut your mouth and stop being so bloody obtuse, the easier it'll be for everyone.'

Lisa's estimation of the man rose in that action, both the message and the delivery impressed her equally and she made a mental note to master that herself in the future. Until now Atkinson had been very quiet, sitting at the back of the room and not getting involved. His presence was required with

SO15 being active in his jurisdiction, but until they had a decent lead on Ali he had been happy to continue working on his phone in the background.

Now he had come alive, and was a welcome addition in Lisa's eyes. Especially after shutting down the idiotic manager so eloquently.

Atkinson turned back to Lisa, 'I'm going to head out and start co-ordinating my response team. They've been on standby at an industrial park up the road, but now that we have a viable suspect, I want them primed and ready ASAP' he said.

He was gone before Lisa could respond, not that she was going to. She was engrossed in the screen. Ali had started to move. He was steering his scooter down the ramp and towards the rear doors of the room. What was he doing? Lisa couldn't see anything that might have spooked him. Will wasn't there yet, he'd stopped in a Starbucks as far as she could see, another bloody snack no doubt. She as going to speak to him about that later, it just wasn't on in the middle of a job. For now, her focus was on the maintenance men, still nowhere to be seen.

She watched the screens intently, not even blinking, as she tried to figure out if the targets movement meant something or nothing. Should she be telling Atkinson to get the response teams to go now, or was he simply getting bored of the view? Was it even *him*? Nothing could be confirmed until Will got up there or the cameras were cleared.

Ali parked up again. The picture wasn't good enough to be sure, but it looked like he was scanning the room. Could it be that this guy was an innocent, just a disabled guy looking for someone? It would be easy to lose someone in these crowds. Her gut said no, he was their man. She just needed to know for certain.

Imran, the officer on the right of the control desk, burst into a loud coughing fit as Ali reached into his pocket and pulled out his phone.

'Ssshhhhh' urged Lisa, trying to concentrate.

Ali seemed to stare at the phone for a few seconds then began punching keys himself.

'Sorry. I think I need some to go and get some water' replied Imran.

Ali folded the phone away and lowered his head, as if in prayer on his scooter.

'Just go Imran. Get some water, just be quick.' barked Hampton.

Imran rose from his chair at the same time as Ali struggled to lift his immense weight from his scooter. Get up he did. And walk perfectly well he could. Other than the initial struggle to get upright, he seemed to move quite easily to Lisa, who's mouth, and eyes, were both opening wide and simultaneous, as realisation landed on her face.

'I fucking *knew* it was him!' cried Lisa, pointing at the screen. She spun around looking for her radio and bumped straight into Imran who was walking behind her.

'Sorry Miss, I...' his words ran dry when the small mobile phone in his breast pocket pinged.

Lisa's look of surprise switched to a frown in a moment as Hampton burst out again. 'I've told you before Imran, no phones allowed in here. Why do you have that?' asked his manager.

'I...I... it's....' stuttered the guard.

Lisa didn't let him finish. She grabbed the phone from his pocket and flipped it open with her right hand in one smooth motion, bunching the knot of the guard's tie, and the surrounding shirt and jumper combo, in her tightly clenched left fist to hold him in place.

'Hey! Let go of my officer' Shouted Hampton.

Lisa ignored him and pressed the envelope that signified text messages and opened the top entry. It was a Samsung smartphone, the kind that showed the entire thread of a conversation on one screen. There were only two messages in the thread. The first from Imran, sent just two minutes earlier;

POLICE WATCHING. UR ON CAMERA.

PICTURE BAD. NOT LONG.

GO NOW OR ABORT

And the reply that had triggered the notification sound as Imran had been heading out of the room;

IMRAN, YOU HAVE HONOURED ALLAH. STALL IF YOU CAN. WE GO NOW. ALLAHU AKBAR

Lisa's blood ran cold. She lifted her face back up to the young man in front of her, ready to give him everything she had. The only thing she gave was a sharp cry, as the full force of his fist connected with her jaw. The punch floored her. For a slight lad, he could hit, and he was fast.

Imran had the knife out of his jacket pocket before the other guard, Jason, could react at all. He'd wanted to buy a Cobra knife for today, a replica of the knife used in the Sylvester Stallone movie of the same name. With its curved blade and sharp steel spikes surrounding the handle guard, it looked incredibly cool, and was popular with the lads that Imran had grown up with. He'd never had one of his own, and Aman had forbidden him getting one now. Instead he'd given the Imran the knife that he held now, that had been stashed in his jacket pocket since this morning. It was as cool as the Cobra, but it wasn't bad. Matt black in colour, the back edge was serrated, the front edge slightly curved and razor sharp. Aman had told him it was a Bowie knife. Imran was grateful for the rubber handle as he gripped it. His hands were sweaty, but it didn't impair his grasp of it at all.

Jason's eyes were still following the woman falling to the floor when the Bowie plunged into his neck. Imran withdrew it with as much force as he'd used to push it through his jugular, sending a spray of arterial blood across the console and CCTV monitors.

When he realised what was happening, Hampton didn't so much scream as weep for help. A pathetic summary of the man's life, Imran thought, as he flicked the Bowie from one hand to the other and moved quickly across the space between him and the flaccid manager, the last man standing.

Hampton was backed away quickly, moving even before Imran had started to close on in. Too quickly, he found out, as he tripped over his own feet and fell to a sweaty heap on the floor. Imran was on him in less than a second.

'Nobody who knows you will blame me for this one,' whispered Imran, his face close to Hampton's as he pushed the tip of the blade through the skin at the top of the man's swollen stomach. He changed angle, moving the hilt down and the blade up, and applied more pressure to drive it under Hampton's sternum, stopping the inane whimpering instantly and tearing through his lungs, piercing his heart. Withdrawing his knife from a dying body for the second time in thirty seconds, Imran panted, 'Allahu Akbar, God is Great.'

He didn't have time to revel in his success. He would be sure to do it later, getting the better of three other people in an enclosed space was something that only the bravest, and smartest, could do. He needed to get the door locked before Atkinson came back, he had to buy his Brothers some more time. Imran danced over the bodies on the floor and engaged the bolts on the inside of the security room door as quietly as he could. He wasn't sure if the Chief was on the other side of the door or not, but was confident that he wouldn't have heard the ruckus if so.

The doors to the room were thick and suppressed most noises. The bolts though were heavy. Imran had been able to hear them opening and closing when he'd been waiting to come into the room in the past. He didn't want to give anything away if he could help it. He needn't have worried too much about that. Just after he slid home the bolt at the bottom of the door, he felt the entire room shake as the first blast went off.

Soon after, there were three more blasts in quick succession. Lights flickered then went out, plaster was shaken loose from the ceiling in the control room in huge chunks, dropping on to Imran and the others in the room, creating a cloud of dust that gave the room a hazy look. It was made more obvious as every light on the desk console was alight with all the warnings, fire alarms and panic alarms going off around the vast shopping centre.

With the main lights out, the console lights vying for attention, and blood still dripping off the monitors, the room looked like the world's most dangerous nightclub.

Imran caught sight of the mayhem on the screens and smiled. There were thousands of people running, screaming, scared for their lives. He watched as all the supposed civility (that Westerners lauded themselves for, especially over the Middle-east, where Imran's family came from, and where he had lost three cousins in bombs dropped in American airstrikes) was thrown out of the window, as they trampled each other to death to survive.

'Go my Brothers. Go and show the world,' He said out loud to himself, 'I'm going to finish this bitch.' He turned away from the screens, drew his knife again, and bent down to where Lisa was lying, unconscious and vulnerable, on the floor.

CHAPTER 25 – THE OUTSIDE

'Sir, with all due respect, why the hell are we sitting on our arses all the way up here?' Commander Charlie Ryan was not the least bit happy at having to stage his tactical team on an industrial estate, a mile away from the target, when there was a perfectly good underground parking facility at the site. They could be seconds, rather than minutes, away from where the shit might go down, but most of all he begrudged sitting out here in the rain and the cold. It was bound to be another false shout, and he getting as fed up of them as he was the weather.

If he were Commander of a Rapid Response team on Costa Teguise, he wouldn't mind being sat outside for hours on end. This was Manchester, it wasn't the same. He couldn't wait for his holiday. He and his Wife, Jackie, were flying out a week from today. Jackie was driving him mad already. The closer it got to flight day, the more stressed out she became. Like a whirlwind that picks up speed with every sleep that came off the countdown calendar she insisted on keeping on the fridge door. By the time they got to one sleep left, she'd be a maniac, doing everything at a hundred miles an hour, leaving a trail of hastily written packing lists in her wake.

'No time for that Ryan. It looks like we're on. We've got a viable target and I need you and your team to get down here now.' barked Chief Atkinson. He was halfway up a stairwell leading from the service tunnel to the precinct above. His cheap mobile phone, that the force had insisted they use in the latest round of cost cutting, meant he struggled to get anything like a decent signal while he was underground.

'Well it's about time Sir.' Ryan snapped out of his slouch, 'We're three minutes out. What's the situation for approach?' asked Ryan.

'At this point we've got no reason to believe there are any external threats, but the whole thing is a bit up in the air at the minute. I'd suggest multiple entry points would be prudent.'

'Agreed Sir. Anything else I need to know?' Ryan insisted on knowing everything possible, about any target they engaged with. Sometimes that involved thorough background work, which he always had his team do. They didn't need to, but he strongly believed that if his team were going to be the ones that faced an immediate threat, then they would be more invested in making sure that they knew everything up front.

In this case, there hadn't been time for that. From the short briefing that he had gotten at 5am that morning, it seemed there wasn't much in the way of background to know.

Before Atkinson could answer, Ryan heard a burst of static on the line, followed by a series of bangs and sharp cracks coming down the line, as if Atkinson had dropped his phone. Two seconds after the first disruption, Ryan heard the explosion for himself, the distance between his team and the site of the explosion delayed the shockwave travelling to his ears.

'Sir! Sir! Chief Atkinson, can you hear me?' Shouted Ryan now, his years of training kicking in and combat mode kicking in light someone had flipped a switch.

More noise down the phone line, as Atkinson found and picked up his phone. 'I'm here Ryan, I'm OK, but you know as much as I do right now Commander. Get here now!'

'Yes Sir!' Ryan snapped shut the phone, tucking it back inside the breast pocket of his jacket. He turned to his team and broke in to a run, heading to his car. He stuck the thumb and forefinger of his left hand in to his mouth and let out an ear-splitting whistle, at the same time as whirling his right hand in the air, with his finger pointing up to the heavy rainclouds above. The universal signal for 'saddle up' was understood by all and his heavily armed team of fourteen, who had each heard and understood the noise just as Ryan had, ran to their own vehicles, ready to do their thing.

They were split across three vehicles. Not the huge armoured Humvee's that were portrayed on TV, but a combination of two Ford Transit vans, kitted out with additional seating in the rear, as well as specially designed secure compartments in the boot area to house their weapons, and a gun-metal grey Volvo V90 with tinted windows and a high performance engine, that meant Ryan would always be the first on scene. Ryan's team were not bothered about turning up in style. Every member of his team was concerned only with doing their job, and doing it perfectly.

All three engines were revving before the last bums had found their seats. Gravel was thrown up from the parking spots they'd been idling in, as accelerator pedals were floored. The adrenaline was flowing for every member of the team, and Ryan suddenly forgot about his holiday. They were a go, and there was no feeling in the world like it.

CHAPTER 26 – THE BROTHERHOOD

It was a good plan. Every Brother knew their job. They had been drilled on it, over and over by Aman, in recent weeks.

When the Whatsapp message came through, they removed their explosive vests and attached them, using the adhesive strips that had been sewn into the back of them, to the strategic points that they'd been assigned. They were all key structural targets; ingress and egress points, load bearing pillars, supporting beams and walls, all chosen to create funnelling channels to drive panicked shoppers through.

Once clear of the area, the Brothers, hiding inside shops and covered positions, triggered their explosives, bringing down entrances and exits to the building, destabilising the outer sections of the building and causing upper levels and ceilings to collapse, setting in motion a chain of events that would leave a painful scar on this city, and country, for a long time to come.

People trapped inside defaulted to survival mode, which meant heading *away* from where the trouble was, going further into the building, looking for another means of escape. They found each route blocked except one.

The Brothers' job was not to wipe out the shoppers completely, merely to drive them inwards, like heavily armed collies herding a flock of terrified, crying sheep to the open expanse of the food hall, in the heart of the structure.

To be sure that they congregated in as large a crowd as possible, each of the Brothers was also carrying an AK47 assault rifle, fully loaded, with four extra thirty-round magazines. In total each of the Brothers had a hundred and fifty rounds to use to steer the crowds toward the centre of the building.

Walking casually, two men from each entryway, shouted loud and sporadically 'Allahu Akbar' as they fired on anyone that wasn't already running in the direction they wanted.

They were relaxed. They had planned for this, trained for it, and it was going exactly to plan. There was no resistance at all, just targets, and just like in the practice sessions they had been having, the targets were proving easy to hit.

Aman had told them to specifically target children and women. Nobody would be affected by videos of men being shot by other men. It happened every day, even here in the UK. It was so common now that it barely made the news any more. Women and children being shot would be a different story. One that would make a lasting mark and mean that they would be remembered forever as heroes of Islam.

The objective was to show the world what would happen if non-believers continued to desecrate and destroy Muslim lands. Aman described to them how news of their victory today would be carried to the world by the power of the internet, and how the world had to see the most shocking images to learn that lesson.

They did not disappoint. Everywhere they turned, there were children with their parents. Within a minute of the last explosion, the concourses were littered with the bodies of children, dead and dying, their mothers close by, having suffered them same way for trying to protect their child.

The Brothers each had a Go-Pro camera mounted on their shirts, streaming every second of the attack live to a site that Aman had set up for the world to see.

The images were bad. Very bad. Horrific. The sounds were worse. Underneath the screaming, shouting, crying, gunfire, and sounds of life expiring in the very worst of ways, was another sound. The sound of the Brothers laughing.

CHAPTER 27 – ERIC MATTHEWS

Seeing Abby again was a shock. Eric told himself that he'd been meaning to find Abby ever since Emily's funeral, but the reality was that he'd been so consumed with everything going on, it just wasn't a priority for him anymore. He'd taken a break from the service after it all happened. It wasn't his choice at first, the mandatory Occupational Health counsellor he'd been sent to had insisted. Eric knew it was the right thing now, looking back. He'd needed that time to get his mind right.

Jenny & Carrie coming along was amazing for him, and totally unplanned. When they were born, it was a chance to close the book on the old Eric. The Eric that was tormented with nightmares of that day, night after night, having the same dream, where he chose to check parked cars instead of choosing to make sure his little girl was safe.

A new book was being written now. He'd gone back to work, committed himself, and gotten the promotion that he'd originally wanted. Finally, he could start making a real difference.

Today was part of that. He'd insisted on being the one that got to take the girls shopping for their ballet shoes, something he'd never done for Emily. Eric was determined to get things right this time and he realised that he had a second chance to do that for Abby too after bumping into him today. Abby had meant a lot to Emily, and Eric felt awful that he hadn't done more for him. He planned to make that right when Abby came round for tea.

Not long after agreeing this silent resolution with himself, he heard the first bomb, and he knew exactly what was happening.

It was only a matter of time before somebody hit in Manchester again, they talked about it all the time in the force. Christ, it was the whole reason that his proposal for a new unit was currently being reviewed by the powers that be.

He grabbed the girls and found cover inside the sports shop they were already in. It didn't sound like the blasts were close by, it was safer to find cover here than take their chances out there. God knows what else was going on.

Eric called it in from his mobile. It wasn't news, there was already a tactical team on route which made him feel a little better. They were the real deal. He knew Charlie Ryan from old, had seen him operate, and that made him more comfortable that taking shelter here was the right choice. He opened his Twitter app. Even the police knew, if you wanted up to the minute information on anything, Twitter was where you went.

His feed was going crazy with news of what was going on, new tweets coming every few seconds. Several of the Tweets carried a link that promised video. Eric clicked into a link, and immediately wished he hadn't. It showed what looked like a live feed being streamed by the shooters themselves.

He'd been expecting jittery camera footage from some millennial type, but instead he was getting a first-person perspective of a full-blown terrorist assault.

He turned the volume down. He didn't want the girls to know what he was watching, Christ, he didn't want to watch it at all. He had to. It was the only way he could tell if they were close to where he was holding his twin baby girls.

CHAPTER 28 – ABDUL

Abdul's task was different to the others. His also involved an explosive vest, but he was not to detonate yet. He'd already attached it to his pillar when the signal first came through. In the chaos nobody would notice it there. The pillar that he was assigned was one of the main weight-bearing pillars for the entryway to the food hall.

His orders were to wait until the hall was packed before detonating, trapping as many people as possible in that space.

Until then he was to act like everyone else. He did that easily, hiding inside the sports shop that he'd bought his overpriced jacket from. Cowering behind a rack of trainers, along with other shoppers and members of staff.

His part would come soon, and he was ready for it.

CHAPTER 29 – WILL

Will brushed the largest chunks of shattered glass out of his hair and got to his feet, looking to the back of the shop to make sure that Neil was OK. Neil signalled he was, he'd been far enough from the shopfront to be unaffected by the result of the blast. Will picked up his Glock, he'd dropped it when the first explosion hit, and forced his way through the mass of customers, those that could still scrambling to their feet, to join Neil.

From a standing position, Will could now see that the casualties were worse than he'd first thought. He felt bad for the people around him, but he couldn't stop to help them now. He checked his phone. No calls from Lisa, things had changed, and she had enough on her plate now without chasing him up. He turned his phone off. He didn't like doing it, ignoring his partner, but he knew she was as safe as she *could* be in the control room, and he had to focus now. The stakes had been raised, massively, and they needed to move now if they were going to get to Ali before anyone else.

Will made to move out but stopped dead before he'd taken a first step. A question jumped out at him, like a beacon shining through fog; With this attack happening now, and Ali having ties to the man, could Al-Naswari be here somewhere himself?

Realising the likelihood of it being true, Will's resolve doubled. HE looked at Neil, 'Ok mate forget the plan, we're winging it from here. Are you still in?' he asked.

'That fucker has just killed even *more* people, no way am I backing out now' replied Neil, checking his safety was off and tucking his spare magazines inside his belt for easy access. All hopes of flying under the radar were already gone so Neil dropped his jacket to give him better access to his MP5. Will did the same.

'Right. Let's go. There's a good chance that Al-Naswari is here himself so eyes peeled, right?'

'Right you are' said Neil, eyes almost sparkling now with their brightness.

'Remember what it was like in Helmand Neil. They needed to have a few people to pull this off and there's far too many targets for them to stop here. There's bound to be hostiles out there and tactical response are not on site yet, so we need to be ready to engage anyone that's carrying.'

'Ok by me' said Neil, making one last check of his spare mags, 'I'm *glad* it's just us. I saw enough blue on blue in Afghan, I don't need to see it in Miss Selfridge's.'

'Stick close to the walls and keep one eye on each other. Fuck knows where they are or what else they're doing. I'll take the far side; you take this side' said Will, absolutely zeroed in on his mission now.

'There you go playing big brother again,' smiled Neil.

The reference brought a smile from Will, as he realised that he might finally get vengeance for Luke. 'You'll thank me later, if you don't get shot in that big fucking spud you call a head.'

'Yeah, yeah. Can we get on with it now?' asked Neil, shoving Will towards the door.

Both men laughed and bumped fists before heading through the space where a window pane used to be, on to the concourse. This was their natural environment, they were comfortable in it. Taking risks and hunting the bad guys is what they signed on for, all those years ago.

Save for the sound of the alarms and the occasional cry, the concourse around them was quiet. Up ahead there was screaming, but it seemed to be getting further away. This was good, it allowed them to move quickly. Neither man spoke aloud, instead used the hand-signals that were a second tongue to anyone that had seen combat.

A combination of closed and open hand gestures, that covered everything from "Stop" and "Go", to "Two enemy ahead, one left, one right". The latter was the signal Will gave to Neil, as they rounded the bend a hundred and twenty yards in, towards the food hall.

Neil got it first time. The language was familiar and comforting to him, but even so he was surprised how quickly it came back after such a long time. The men agreed to move closer before engaging, there were clearly civilians further ahead and any missed shots would likely fire into the crowd.

They had to speed up, the men in front were firing what sounded like AK-47's at unsuspecting shoppers and needed to be stopped quickly. The noise from the alarms covered any noise they might make, so they broke into a run to cover the ground faster.

When they were within fifty feet, Neil gave the signal to stop. Both men hunkered down into firing position, one knee on the ground, the other foot planted firmly in front. To avoid giving anything away to any other possible shooters, Will signalled to fire at the same time. Neil counted them down from three, two, one...

Both soldiers hit their mark first time, although Will's target didn't go down quite as cleanly as Neil's. Will was up and closing the fifty-foot gap to his man before the report from their shots had finished echoing around the high ceilings, three storeys up. He kept his weapon trained on target, ready to put another round in him if he showed any signs of recovering. He didn't. As Will got closer he saw that, while he didn't land an immediately fatal shot, his man was bleeding out rapidly from a fresh hole in his neck. Will picked up the man's rifle and slung it over his own back. No point leaving a perfectly good gun in someone else's hands.

Neil caught up and inspected his own man. 'That's a perfect ten on the gun range for me. How about you?'

'A strong eight.' Replied Will.

'Ha! I bet you're glad I'm here now then, cockeye' Neil sniggered.

'Shut up knobhead!' laughed Will. 'And get moving. I can still hear shooting. We've got work to do, and God knows how long we've got left to get Ali before the tactical boys get in here.'

CHAPTER 30 – LISA

With the door locked and the attack already underway, Imran's main job was done, yet he had no intention of running away.

That had been the plan at first. He was going to alert Aman if needed, excuse himself from the control room and head on upstairs to join his Brothers. Instead the SO15 bitch had cottoned on to him earlier than planned, ruining his part in things. But no matter. He'd been more useful staying here, stopping them from getting word to the outside about what was going on.

Moreover, he now had sole control of the buildings camera systems, so even if the Police Chief, or that dickhead Will Grant, did get through to the police outside, they had no way of directing them to where his Brothers were. Imran had come into this knowing exactly what to expect, and what his fate would be. In that respect, everything was going to plan. All he had to do now was hold tight, watch it all unfold. No matter how things unfolded from here, there were only two possible outcomes for him, glorious martyrdom and a warm welcome in paradise, or capture, and prison for the rest of his life.

Prison was the least preferred option, but there were still benefits to be had from it. For a start, prison in the U.K. was a joke. He was a smart guy. He'd already looked up various human rights lawyers that he knew he could use, not only to make sure he got a comfy ride in prison, but to help make as much noise as possible publicly, to encourage his Brothers to continue the Jihad, including suing the government at every possible turn.

Imran had followed the extensive news coverage of how Michael Adebolajo, despite being sentenced to life for killing Lee Rigby, had filed suit for compensation against the prison service after he'd been attacked while locked up.

It was all over the newspapers and T.V. for weeks. He'd even been granted legal aid to pay for his lawyers! Imran knew he could use a situation like that to even greater effect, to get the message out to the entire world, and be praised as a hero for doing it. The irony of it all amused Imran. It could never happen under Shariah law. Any country that brushed aside the hurt done to its own people, for fear of offending others, deserved everything it got in his opinion.

Paradise and the glory of martyrdom was still his preferred outcome. He'd figure out a way to get out of here and join the fight soon enough. For now, this was where he'd stay, and why not have some fun while he was here?

It was just him and the woman in here now. Nobody coming in or out. She was completely at his mercy. She was fit too. He'd been checking her out all morning. Tight jeans sculpted to the toned curves of her calves, and thighs. Great arse. Slim, but not flat chested by any means. Her top was less tight than her jeans, but even so Imran knew there was a great pair under there.

He'd never had sex with a white girl before. Lots of his friends had. Where he'd grown up, the lads on the estate had made a game of it. It was a well-known truth amongst the Asian boys in Bradford that white girls around there were slags, and would do anything for a bit of weed, or even a bag of chips. They kept a tally of how many "Whiteys" they bagged. It was a bragging game, and they loved to play it.

If he was going to paradise today, then why not bag himself one before he goes?

He nudged his foot into Lisa's ribs to see if she was stirring yet. She'd still been unconscious when he first grabbed her by the hair in the aftermath of the explosions. He was impressed by his own strength, one punch and she'd been out for about 5 minutes. He didn't want to kill her while she was out, what was the point? It was time for her to wake up now though, she had something else to do before she died.

She still wasn't stirring. How hard had he hit her? Was she even still alive? Imran dropped to one knee to get a better view of whether she was breathing. He'd have checked her pulse, if only he knew how. He couldn't see if she was breathing from where he was and leaned down further, putting both hands on the floor in front of him, the knife flat on the floor under his right hand.

He put his ear to her chest. He could feel the warmth of her breasts against his ear, growing excited to see if they looked as good as they felt. Straining to hear, he leaned further forward.

That was Lisa's moment. She'd had to take a big chance and play the situation out. She'd never lost consciousness for a moment. It would take a lot more than a punch from this scrawny prick to take her out, although the shock of how fast he'd moved had surprised her for sure. The way that she'd landed meant that reaching her service weapon was impossible, at least without giving away that she was awake. Knowing now how fast he could move, she knew it was a gamble to go for the gun in such a small room. He could be on her in no time, and with the Bowie knife in his hand she didn't like the odds. Now she'd played dead long enough, she wasn't going to get a chance as good as this again.

Lisa lifted her head quickly and latched her teeth on to Imran's cheek, biting down as hard as she could. She shot her right hand out to grab the wrist of the arm leaning on the knife, conscious that it was still a danger to her.

Imran screamed in pain and moved to stab her. He couldn't. With all his weight bearing down on his wrists, and her hand also holding his in place, he couldn't move it. His left hand was still free, so he used it to punch her again. He could only get a shot to her temple, but it wasn't enough. She wasn't letting go, like a Doberman welcoming a burglar, she was locked on him. He could feel her teeth sinking deeper into his flesh. He punched her again, and again, on the temple, desperate to make her release him before she took his cheek clean off.

As she wriggled around, following Imran's movements to keep the pressure in her jaw high, Lisa worked her left-hand underneath her back to free her gun. Imran continued to strike her on the side of the head, but the shots were like being hit by a child, no power at all. Regardless, after the

132

fourth punch she relaxed her jaw and released him, careful to keep a tight grip on the hand holding the knife.

She needed the extra space to get her shot off safely, without risking hurting herself in the process. As Imran's head recoiled at being released, bearing his own teeth in anger and pain, Lisa rolled thirty degrees onto her right side, and brought her left-hand up, and round, in a wide arc.

The adrenaline surging through Imran was like nothing he'd felt before. He couldn't feel the pain coming from his half-chewed cheek, he felt only rage. How dare this woman attack *him*? As he leaned back, ready to lunge down and kill this woman, he felt invincible, he was back in control.

The arc of Lisa's arm movement finished, with the muzzle of her 9mm beretta resting perfectly on Imran's temple. She'd already flicked the safety off as she'd brought her arm around and fired as soon as she felt the resistance of his head against her barrel.

Imran felt nothing more.

Lisa let out a heavy sigh as she shoved Imran's lifeless body away from her. She'd already lost too much time, she was kicking herself for playing dead while above her in the Trafford Centre, people were in real trouble. She knew she had no other choice, but the whole time she'd been lying there with her eyes almost closed, she was thinking about the footfall counter on the console. God knows what was happening up there. Questions filled her head; Was this Al-Naswari or a coincidence? How was Aman Ali connected to this? How the *fuck* had they not known anything about an attack? The one that got her moving again; How many innocent people had already lost their lives while she was only pretending to have lost hers?

Lisa scrambled up, her heels slipping on the broken plaster that was scattered around her until she got a foot in the space that her prone body had kept clean. Her first task was to get a handle on the situation. She was in the right place for that, she had all the cameras in the centre at her disposal right here. Looking up at the monitors, she realised there was a problem.

All the screens were black. There wasn't a single image on any of them. The console lights had all gone out too. While lying on the floor, she'd seen the glow from them dancing off the walls and ceilings, as if she was at a party, now the only dim glow in the room came from the emergency lights above the door.

They'd all been on before her struggle with Imran. Her best guess was that the round she'd sent into his brain had gone straight through and found its final resting spot in the servers underneath the console desk. Presumably, that had fried the system altogether. Great.

'Now what?' she asked of nobody. 'Shit. Will!' she answered herself, remembering that her partner was out there by himself. She grabbed for her phone and ran to get out of the still stifling room.

CHAPTER 31 – THE BRIMSONS

'I'm scared Dad. What's happening?' Josh couldn't stay quiet, no matter how much his mum and dad told him to. 'I want to go home.'

'Josh, baby, please. We've got to stay quiet. It's like hide and seek ok? We don't want to be found, do we?' Karen was doing her best to make the boy less scared. She figured that making it into an adventure for him was the best bet. 'It's just like in Spiderman. The superheroes will be here soon, and they'll take care of us. We just have to stay here, and stay as quiet as we can until then, ok?'

They had been sitting on a bench in the concourse eating their lunch when the first bomb had gone off. They couldn't get a seat in the food court in the end. The queues for food were so long, by the time they'd all been served, all the tables were full. Instead they carried their lunch with them a while and perched on the first bench they found. Not enough room for them all to sit, Simon stood facing them while he ate.

When the first blast hit, a cloud of confusion seemed to descend all around them. People stopped in their tracks. They turned to ask each other what had happened. Should they be worried? Simon knew straight away, and he wasted no time.

He grabbed Josh up off the seat, holding him on his waist while he pulled Karen and Sophie up out of their seats too. 'Go! Go! Over there,' he pointed to the Lush shop, behind where they were sitting. 'Get in there now. Go straight to the storeroom out the back.'

They ran through the small shop, barely noticing the pungent smells of perfumed soaps, candles, and bath bombs, all kept out on display to tempt people in with their powerful scents.

The young girl working the till saw them push their way through the door to the storeroom and started to shout after them that they couldn't go through there. The second wave of explosions changed her mind, and she followed them through the door instead. The few other customers that had been in the shop at the time headed out of the shop instead, on to the concourse.

Simon looked around for a way out. Maybe a loading bay, or even better a lift. There was none. He asked the girl, but she told him that all their deliveries came in the front door. There was no other way out.

'Shit! Ok, we've got to barricade ourselves in then. Help me. Get all those boxes and stack them against the door.' Simon started to move quickly. Karen was huddling the kids into her and didn't want to leave them.

'What's happening Simon?' she asked.

'It's terrorists. I saw someone dodgy in the food hall earlier and reported it to security. I don't know if It's related, but it'd be a hell of a coincidence if not'

'Fucking hell, are you serious?'

'Listen to those blasts babe, I'd say they're serious, wouldn't you?' Simon stacked the last few boxes against the door. There wasn't many. Maybe ten boxes all in all. The barricade might hold a light attempt to get through the door, but it wouldn't do much to stop a determined person getting in. It would have to do.

On any other day, Karen would have loved being stuck in this shop. Smelling the various fragrances, making the most of the testers that were available. This was one of her favourite shops. The smells reminded her of being younger, going shopping with her friends, being carefree.

Now her only care in the world was getting her kids out of here alive.

CHAPTER 32 – AMAN ALI

After sending the message to begin, Aman also had a role to play. It was tricky, he had to disable the emergency door at the back of the food hall, closing the exit for anyone that might head for it.

He had to move quickly, not easy for a big guy but timing was everything at this stage. If he didn't go until the first blast went off, it would look to anyone else that he was trying to open the doors, simply the first person there. In truth, he would be disabling the doors using a pair of nickel-plated rigid handcuffs secured to both handles.

He'd considered going more hi-tech for this part of the plan. In the past he'd masterminded a robbery which involved the use of phosphorous poured inside a heavy-duty lock. Once lit it didn't burn as hot as other incendiary materials, but it did melt to liquid, which in that instance was perfect. The hot liquid flowed through the entire locking mechanism, destroying it from the inside.

That wouldn't work here. He didn't want to destroy the lock completely, that might make the doors easier to open. He'd thought about flash welding the hinges, stopping the doors from opening either way, but decided against that for timing. He'd need a lot more time to do that effectively and the effort needed to source a concealable welding kit was significant. All these things had to be considered in planning.

It was that balance of effort versus reward that brought him back to the simplest solution in the end. The handcuffs would need to be removed either with the key, which would not be available, or with significant power tools. The odds of anyone having those on their person, or within reach in the ten minutes or so that he needed to keep them in place, were low enough to be an acceptable risk.

It was also very quick to apply them. It took him less than two seconds to fish them from his inside coat pocket and snap them on to the shafts of the handles. To anyone stood behind him it looked like he was simply trying to open the doors.

They would still open, and did, he had to sell the lie for anyone that happened to be watching, but the reinforced metal cuffs stopped the opened doors creating any more than a gap of three inches.

The window was made of reinforced safety glass. Even if it were smashed, it would only shatter and continue to hold in place. Good old British health and safety laws required that to be the case because of the size of the panes.

None of this meant that there was *no* way out. Enough sustained effort would of course break the door open, or smash the glass panes through. In planning, previous experience of how the human mind works when in panic had given Aman confidence that one failed attempt to get through would be enough to cause any would be escapees to quit and look for other options.

He didn't need it to hold for long, just enough time for the crowds from the other areas of the shopping centre to be herded into the main room. Once there, the explosion from his mobility scooter would take care of anyone within a twenty-metre circumference. The ball bearings wrapped around the explosive core of the machine would be propelled outwards in a three-hundred-and-sixty- degree radius, at up to two thousand miles per hour.

One steel ball flying at that speed would rip through a dozen people in a straight line as if they were made of paper, and that's before any ricochet effect sent it off in a new direction. He had five hundred of them covering every angle.

CHAPTER 33 – HAMZA AL-NASWARI

Hamza was taking a risk being here himself. Not something he would normally do but his options were few, it was becoming harder to recruit after the fall of Daesh. Although he'd gotten enough disillusioned young men on board for this mission, and they were so far proving loyal to Aman, he couldn't trust any of them to pull it off without his oversight.

Abdul would not blow the pillar covering the entrance to the food hall until Aman gave the direct order. That had been made very clear, and that kept Hamza safe. What Abdul didn't know was that he would be getting that order only when Hamza was well clear of the blast radius.

Hamza didn't fully trust Abdul. He might have been Aman's nephew, in a manner of speaking, but he was also his parent's Son which meant he couldn't be relied on. Abdul's Father was a liability. Hamza had never met the man in person, but Aman had spoken with him on the phone occasionally, when the two sisters would phone each other. It was after one of those phone calls that Aman found out about his betrayal.

Nayna had called her sister to talk and, as always, Aman had been given every detail after the call ended. Ahmed had confided in his wife that he had been approached by Hezbollah to do some work for them. It wasn't the kind of proposition you turned down, without fear of reprisal. Ahmed had decided to go along with their plan for the sake of his family's safety. He had also told his wife that he was planning to report everything to the American Embassy once the work was done, in the hope of getting his family safe passage to the U.S.

Hamza couldn't allow that. He made calls of his own, to contacts he had within Hezbollah from his days in Lebanon. Two days later, Ahmed was killed.

Hamza had to be careful when Ahmed's widow and Son moved to Manchester. He didn't know for sure that Nayna had suspicions, but Nayna had known that it was only she whom her husband had confided in, and she had only confided in her sister, who would never betray her trust.

Hamza ordered one of his men to follow the women whenever they were out away from Aman. When one of them told him that he'd caught Nayna coming out of a police station, he knew that he had to act.

Hamza made sure that Aman was seen at the mosque at the same time the car mowed them down, so that when the inevitable questions came, he could respond with honest answers and lots of witnesses. His alibi also made sure that Abdul never questioned anything about the accident.

Aman's grace in looking after the boy since then would be repaid today. Aman had slowly but surely radicalised Abdul. It wasn't hard. After his girlfriend Emily was killed in the IRA explosion in Manchester, Abdul retreated into himself.

He rarely left the house, lost his job, became depressed. From that point on Aman had all the time in the world to turn him. The process was terrifyingly simple and devastatingly effective. Hamza had used it all over the world with magnificent results. It worked with groups almost as well as individuals.

He had recruited an entirely family once, back in Syria, from Grandmother down to Grandchildren.

All it took was one event, one grievance, that Hamza could twist and manipulate to his own ends. The loss of Emily, his Mother, and Father, practically guaranteed Abdul would be compliant.

It started with cutting off outside contact and, once again, Abdul had done all the hard work himself, losing his job and falling out of touch with his football friends.

Once Aman was Abdul's primary contact, he would gradually start to influence his thinking. 'You are a victim Abdul.' 'It's not your fault Abdul, it's their fault.' 'They did this to you Abdul.'

Phrases like this were a lifeline to the person, or people, struggling with grief. It gave them something to cling to in their darkest moments, and that darkness made them even more believable.

Hamza knew, and so Aman knew, that once a target believed this new perspective, that they were indeed the victim of a malignant oppressor, it was simply a case of broadening the perception of that oppressor to make sure that any possible threats to the plan such as friends or work colleagues, those that could reignite the target's social interactions, were also viewed as the enemy. This was key to ensuring success. From there it was just a matter of pushing the thought of retribution as a righteous act.

Terrifyingly simple. Devastatingly effective.

Aman had the same deadly skills as Hamza in this area and was patient and thorough to bring Abdul over to his cause.

Abdul's death today as a martyr for the Jihad would make the time that Aman had invested in the boy more than worthwhile, and would tie off the last loose end connecting Hamza and Aman with the deaths of his Mother and Aunt.

CHAPTER 34 – ERIC MATTHEWS

The video must have been taken down. Eric had been watching for the last ten minutes, trying to track where the attackers were in relation to his own position, but now the screen had turned to black and the feed was gone. He assumed the tactical team were doing their thing. Before the picture cut out, he'd just one terrorist gunned down on screen. He couldn't quite make out the officer, but it had to be Ryan's men.

Eric's brain was racing. It was too much of a coincidence that he'd bumped into Abby today and now this was happening. He didn't know what to do.

He let out a sigh, slipped the phone back into his pocket and cuddled the girls closer to him. Getting the girls out of here was his first thought, he would deal with the rest later. He just had to focus on them.

Eric hoped that the officer he'd seen on camera was OK. He was sure he would be, they worked in teams and he was sure he'd caught the reflection of another guy in a shop window before the picture cut out, standard assault formation.

CHAPTER 35 – WILL

The food hall was seventy feet ahead on the right. Will and Neil were huddled in the doorway of a sports shop. Shots could still be heard, coming from two directions. One around the corner to the left. Judging by the sound, the shooters were about fifty feet away and advancing closer. The second shooters were directly ahead. Will could see people running towards them from the concourse on the other side of the food hall.

Will had suspected that this was their plan. Seal the exits, drive everyone inwards from the outermost points of the centre and then, once they were all gathered centrally, Will assumed there'd be a secondary blast, even bigger than the first ones. Will explained his theory to Neil while they took cover in the doorway.

'Hang on, did you say that Ali was disguising himself by using a mobility scooter?' asked Neil.

'Yes I....Fuck! That's the bomb!'

'That's the bomb. They did similar things in Kandahar, using wheelchairs to carry IEDs into crowds and public places' Neil recalled.

'Shit. There must be over a hundred thousand people in here.' Will massaged his forehead with the fingertips of both hands. A habitual thing that he did when he was thinking under pressure. 'and we can't even get to Ali with those other shooters out there, never mind stop a fucking bomb.'

'The way I see it,' said Neil, calmly now, it was no time to play the fool, 'we have to take the shooters first, otherwise we run the risk of being blindsided. I know they're not the main target, but we won't get any closer to Al-Naswari if we're both shot in the fucking back.'

'Yeah you're right' said Will. He wiped both hands on his jean legs to dry them. It'd been a while since he'd been this close to proper action, his hands were sweaty. 'OK, so we head for cover by the shop on the corner there,' he pointed across the way, 'the shooters aren't far away and getting closer, so we'll have to be quick. You ready?'

'Ever ready, like the batteries' replied Neil, the fool creeping back in a bit now that Will had come down a few degrees from boiling point. He was in his element. He knew it was serious, and dangerous, but this was what he lived for.

No count this time, they just ran. Full speed across the width of the walkway. They could hear the shooters shouting now. They couldn't be more than fifteen feet from the corner. They'd be in sight in seconds.

Will might have been rusty with his shooting, but he was fitter and faster than Neil, making the cover of the pillar on the corner a full second before Neil did. The pillar was just wide enough for them both if they bunched together. The shooters were very close now, they had to go back to hand signals,

Two shooters.

Count of 3.

Me left.

You right.

I take the nearest

Neil smiled at the admission of his superior marksmanship, that Will's signalling had confessed, and nodded. Will gave the count and they went in unison.

Neil's guy was thirty feet away, on the other side of the walkway, his attention on a woman crawling a few feet in front of him. He was grinning, like it was a game. Stalking behind her as she scrambled to reach what Neil thought must be her Son. He couldn't have been more than three years old. Crying his eyes out and calling for his Mummy with his arms reaching out to her.

Neil had seen enough. He took a breath, lined up his sights, and sent the guy flying through the window of the shop behind him with a short burst of three, well aimed rounds to the side of the head.

Will's target was a lot closer than he'd expected. As he rounded his side of the pillar, the barrels of their guns collided with each other, pushing both upwards. Will reacted faster than his target, bringing his knee up in to the man's rib cage, sending him down onto his knees. The guy kept a grip on his rifle as he went down and threw himself back towards Will, slamming the stock into the side of Will's knee.

Will's leg buckled and he went down. His H&K coming loose from the shoulder strap and skittering away, across the concourse floor. He struggled frantically to get his Glock loose from his waistband. His longline T-Shirt was still covering it, making it a harder task than it should be, and maybe costing Will his life.

He had to move, or he'd be dead. He fell on to his back and began rolling as fast as he could to find cover. Not fast enough. The guy with the AK-47 had found his balance again and was drawing down on Will.

Will closed his eyes tight and waited for the shots to land. Behind closed eyes, he saw himself and Luke as kids, playing soldiers in the woods behind Will's house. It was the happiest memory that he had, and he was glad it was going to be his last.

CHAPTER 36 – THE OUTSIDE

There was dust, rubble, and glass everywhere. Commander Charlie Ryan, and the assault team that followed him in the first Transit, could see it before they even pulled to a stop outside the entryway to the east of the building. Plumes of smoke were clearly visible on their way in, from over a mile away, but they weren't heavy, and round here that could mean anything. For near on a year there'd been a trend, amongst the scummier elements of the city, to set fire to cars in crowded car parks. In the last 3 months alone, there had been five such instances at this very shopping centre.

It was clear that this wasn't one of those occasions as the swung to a stop, angled to the kerb a few feet from where the doors used to be. The concrete columns, that were recently supporting the slab and glass roofing structure that marked the entrance to the Trafford Centre, were now nothing more than chunks of broken rock all over the pavement. There was a newly laid, broken glass carpet covering every part of the pavement visible under rock. Car alarms were sounding, the vehicles closest to the building had lost their windows in the blast.

More worrying for Ryan, the entrance itself was gone. There was no way through. He radioed through to Beta team, who he'd sent to the Western entrance.

'Beta team, this is Alpha. Our entry is shut off. We have to find another way in. Don't wait for us, get in there.'

'Copy Alpha. We've got the same problem. They've done a real number on these doors, the whole area is a mess. I can't see a safe way in'

'Shit,' muttered Ryan, careful not to broadcast it over the airwaves. They couldn't risk breaching one of the fire doors nearby, not without a clear view of what was on the other side. Now that they knew explosives were in play, he was not going to risk any member of his team on a blind entry, especially not one that was so obviously the next best choice. If he were a bomber, he would absolutely have trapped those doorways.

'Ok Beta. Have a look around, see if you can find an entry point with line of sight. I've got blueprints in the car, I'll work out secondary access options and come back to you.'

CHAPTER 37 – LISA

The heels had to come off once again. As Lisa burst out of the control room, they'd been kicked off her feet, but instead of them landing against the opposite wall as they normally might, she kicked them back inside the control room before the door slammed shut. These were Michael Kors, patent leather heels, brand new, at least £175 worth, and she didn't want to come back down here later to find them on the feet of some opportunistic cleaning lady. She was careful not to kick them *too* far inside, she also didn't want to have to clean blood off them.

Her head was starting to hurt from the punches she'd taken from Imran. She told herself he wasn't strong enough to knock her out, so they couldn't hurt that much. Knowing that was enough to distract from the pain.

The lift was waiting on another floor, and she didn't want to wait for it to arrive. She had to keep moving, to feel like she was doing something, she couldn't leave Will up there by himself.

She took the stairs two and three at a time, all her sessions in the gym doing box jumps finally paying off. Halfway up the second flight of stairs, she ran in to CSI Atkinson, quite literally. She sent him crashing down on his backside, while she scrabbled to reach the handrail to keep herself upright.

'Bloody hell, you scared me' said Atkinson.

'Shit. Sorry Chief. Are you ok?' Lisa panted. She was out of breath and shaking. 'What's going on up here?'

'Haven't you been watching on the cameras?' he asked, pulling himself up using the handrail on his left.

'Cameras are down. One of the guards was a plant and it all went to shit in that room. It's a long story that I don't have time for now, without being rude. Basically, everyone's dead.'

'Everyone? The guard too?' asked Atkinson, struggling to get his hear around what he'd just heard.

'Oh god yes. I made sure of that.'

It took Atkinson a few seconds to respond to Lisa's last comment, the bluntness of it something that he wasn't used to hearing in his usual circles. 'OK, well that couldn't be helped, I suppose.' Atkinson let out a heavy sigh.

He was a fast-tracked officer. Brought in for his academic talent, rather than his policing experience. This kind of thing was well beyond his training, and life experience. What he did have in abundance was common sense and it was this that told him to forget about jurisdiction, rank, and anything else that had no meaning in this stairwell, and to defer to Lisa for leadership. 'I've mobilized the tactical response teams, but they're having trouble getting into the building. This was well-planned, they've covered every ground level entry point.' This was said more with Atkinson's usual pace, like a briefing, or a press conference, just the facts. 'The tactical commander is looking at options to ingress via the roof, but explosions have compromised the integrity of the structure, they need to find the right point of entry. I'm waiting on a call from him to tell me next steps. In the meantime, what do you need?'

'I don't suppose you're armed, are you?' asked Lisa, recognising the need in his voice for her to take control.

'I'm afraid not. This uniform is purely for decoration, at least as far as the reality of today goes.'

'Yeah, I thought it was a long shot.' Lisa pushed her way past Atkinson on the stairs, squeezing through the gap on the handrail side and pivoting back to continue talking, 'I've got to get going. My partner is out there, and I need to make sure he's OK. Not to mention stopping these bastards, if we can. If you're not armed, then I'd rather you weren't with me. No offence, I just can't be babysitting you if it kicks off.'

149

'Fine by me. I do want to help though. Perhaps I can come up and try to tend to the wounded? I've had extensive first aid training, and it doesn't look like we'll be getting ambulances in here any time soon.'

'Good on you Sir. Ok this way,' Lisa took the lead. It was only one more flight up to the shopping level. She opened the door a crack, enough to get a view left and right. Once she was happy it was clear, she stepped through. She pointed Atkinson to the left, where there were bodies strewn across the floor. Some moving, some dead still. She went right, not saying another word to the Chief. There was no more to say.

She didn't have time to be careful, she'd have to shift if she was going to do anything useful. Bare feet helped, she could move fast and nimble without having to worry about making noise. Will could be anywhere up here, but if she knew him at all, she knew that he wouldn't be hiding. He'd be trying to stop this fucking mess.

Her suspicion was confirmed when she came across two dead shooters after just a few seconds of running. Good! Will had gotten this far unscathed at least, she thought as she picked up the pace with renewed energy.

More bodies, all over the floor of the concourse. Left, right, inside shops too. She must have passed over a hundred, maybe closer to two hundred. Eight out of every ten seemed to be women and children. How sick was this Ali guy? How the hell had they never heard of him before?

The further she went, the was worse the damage became. She'd been witness to some bad things in her life, but this was something different, it didn't seem real to her.

Running through this massacre, jumping over bodies, seeing the pain on the faces of those that weren't quite dead, it was like she was in a horror movie. She couldn't hold back the tears. Her vision blurred making it hard to see what was up ahead. Her hearing though was OK. She heard a short burst of three quick-fire rounds, that had to be a sub-machine gun, just around the corner up ahead. 'Fuck!' she uttered, realising that her 13 round Browning hi-power was no match for firepower on that scale.

She'd kept the Browning even though the standard issue for the service was changed to Glock some time ago. She preferred the feel of the older weapon, but found herself realising suddenly that, after the incident on Moss Side, she'd hoped to never have to fire it again. She'd even been avoiding the gun range. Christ, how much did she regret that now?

She slowed to a jog and got close to the wall on the left for cover. If these arseholes had machine guns, she'd need as much of that as possible.

Rounding the corner, she had almost no time to process what was in front of her. Will was there, on his back on the floor, a guy wearing a tactical vest stood over him, bringing his barrel to bear. She didn't think about it, she reacted, firing three fast shots.

All three flew true, only a few feet over Will's vulnerable body, two of them hitting the shooter centre-mass, right in the vest, sending him staggering backwards. The third got him in the throat and took him down, just in time, as he let go two shots from his own rifle on the way down. They went harmlessly astray, smashing into the floor of the concourse, sending chips of marble-effect, polished concrete up into the air.

Lisa ran over to Will and helped him to his feet. He was covered in concrete chips which Lisa brushed off him.

'At least it's not more fucking pie crumbs' she said with a smile.

'Not this time, no. Thank you Lisa. I thought I was fucked there. I owe you.' Will wrapped his arms around Lisa and gave her a quick hug.

'Come on, in here quick' Lisa said, pulling Will into the Ann Summers shop behind them. He let himself be pulled along by her. He was still in soldier mode and felt a strong urge to make an inappropriate comment about where she was taking him, but then remembered about Neil.

Looking over to where Neil had been taking cover when Lisa arrived, he had time for one more hand-signal before he disappeared into the shop. Neil caught it, nodded, and turned to make his way further up the concourse.

CHAPTER 38 – ABDUL

Still no message from Aman. Abdul held the phone in his hand, pretending to dial out, like he was having trouble getting through to anyone, in case someone was watching him. They weren't. They were too busy, being scared out of their minds. Most of the shoppers hiding amongst the racks of shoes were teenagers. Girls crying and sobbing, trying to hold it together, while being shushed by boys and the handful of grown-ups that were also there. Two of the boys had manoeuvred themselves to the end of the racks, trying to stick their hands around the edge and film what was happening outside. What were they thinking?

Abdul continued scanning the faces, subtly, making sure that nobody was paying him more attention than they should be under the circumstances. Most weren't. One was.

Emily's dad, Eric, was in here with him. He sat on the floor behind an Adidas display, twin girls wrapped in his arms. Now, sitting here looking at them, Abdul could see the resemblance, it was startling. Two identical doubles of Emily herself. He wondered why he hadn't seen it earlier. Maybe he just hadn't wanted to.

Whenever he thought of Emily, all he saw was her hand slipping out of his, as the shrapnel from the truck bomb took her away from him. It wasn't a memory he clung to deliberately, he just couldn't lose it, no matter how he tried. Maybe that was the real reason that he'd agreed to go along with Aman's plan today. Maybe he'd just had enough of seeing people slip away, Emily, his Mum, his Dad. Why was everyone he loved taken from him?

He turned away from Eric and continued pretending to press buttons on his phone.

A minute passed. Then two. Then five. Still nothing from Aman. All the while, he could hear gunshots ringing around from the walkways outside the shop. They were deafening, echoing around the shop. Something about the acoustics of having racking mounted on the walls perhaps. It was so loud that he didn't hear Eric shuffle across to where he was sitting. It was only when he spoke, close to Abdul's ear, that he registered someone was there.

'Abby.'

'Fuck!' said Abdul, jumping almost out of his skin. 'What are you doing? Get back to your family.'

'I can't. This is important. Abby, tell me the truth, is it your Uncle doing this?'

'What? Aman? No don't be ridiculous.'

'Abby. The thing that I wanted to talk to you about, I think your Uncle killed your Mum. I'm sorry to just spit it out but if your Uncle is behind this, and you're involved in any way, then you have to hear it now before you do anything you'll regret.'

'I'm not involved, and my Uncle did not ha....'

'Abby, listen to me!' Eric shouted, cutting him off mid-sentence. 'Your Mum and her sister came to see me at the station, two days before they were killed. They wanted to talk about someone called Hamza Al-Naswari. They said that he was a terrorist and that they had information about how he had arranged to have your father killed,' Eric continued, 'we didn't have much of a computer system back then, so I took some details and said I'd get someone to go round and see them at home. They both panicked, they didn't want anyone coming to the house. They said it wasn't safe there. Your mum said she was going to take you and her sister and go somewhere safe. Then she was going to call me, and we were going to arrange another meeting. Abby, she never called. And she clearly didn't get you out of there.'

Eric took a breath. Abdul was still avoiding eye contact, so Eric moved his face to get in his eyeline again.

'Abby, your Uncle is dangerous. I think he killed your Mother, your Father, and your Aunt. Now this is happening. I couldn't save your Mum, Abby, and I'm so sorry for that. But my Emily, my Emily loved you and I know, I just know, that if I let you do this now, Emily would never forgive me.'

Both men sat there looking at each other. The silence broken eventually by the chime of Abdul's phone.

CHAPTER 39 – LISA & WILL

Will kicked himself. Literally stamped on his own foot. How the hell had he not figured out that Imran was part of this? The snidey little fucker. Will should've sniffed him out, way before he'd had a chance to lay hands on Lisa.

'I'm sorry Lisa. I left you in there to deal with that by yourself.'

'Don't be daft, you were doing the right thing. The only thing you could do. You weren't to know.'

Will felt the stabbing pain of guilt hit him hard in the chest. He hadn't been doing the right thing, had he? Maybe it was right for Luke, for the sense of duty that he felt, his responsibility to take revenge, but it damn sure wasn't the right thing for Lisa.

He wanted to tell her everything. Right here and now. Not just about Al-Naswari and Luke, but about how he felt about her too.

It was a strange reaction to a near death moment, wanting to confess everything. He'd seen it happen to others in his days in the army. He'd been out on patrol in Derry in the early 90's, part of a team of four, including Lieutenant Matt Woodford. Matt was the dog of the unit. Whenever they were stationed away, and sometimes when they weren't, Matt was chasing women. On the odd occasion he couldn't catch a willing one, he was more than happy to rent one for a while. This changed Will's opinion of the guy, it was common for guys in the forces, but he didn't agree with using prostitutes, and Matt was not someone that he kept in touch with after he left the unit.

He did still share the story of Matt's night in Derry whenever he could though. It tickled Will whenever he thought of it.

They'd somehow managed to wander right into the middle of a feud between the INLA and the IPLO, two warring factions of paramilitaries, at least he *thought* that was who it was, who could keep track of all the bloody names? Will knew he probably got the names mixed up over the years, but it didn't matter to the story. What mattered was when they'd been pinned down behind a burned-out Ford Escort, Matt had decided to be a hero and break cover to get the rest of the unit out. He ran to the building over the road, under heavy fire, which *was* heroic as it went. What he didn't know was he'd ran straight in to a building where a gunman from one of the two warring groups was also taking cover.

Next thing Will and the rest of the team knew, Matt was being walked out of the building with a gun to the back of his head. He would've been a goner, if the dickhead holding him hadn't shown off and made him kneel before shooting. As soon as Matt started to move down to his knees, a 9mm round ventilated the forehead of the guy stood behind him. The unit got clear of the trouble after that and beat feet back to base, leaving the two groups to wipe each other out if that was what they wanted.

Once back, Matt got straight on the phone to his wife. Overcome with what Will could only assume was guilt, Matt had spilled it all down the phone line. All the women, all the lies, everything. Matt swore that confessing everything was the best thing he'd ever done, that he and his Wife were rock solid after that, promising never to betray her again. He rotated out two weeks later to find his Wife gone, his house on the market, and his prized vinyl collection, worth thousands of pounds he would tell anyone that listened, including a pristine copy of the White Album, melted into a black heap on the front lawn.

Will found that hilarious. In his book, anyone that could treat the person that they'd vowed to honour that way deserved everything they got. Will had seen for himself what happened when someone was unfaithful. Not in his own love life, although there were a few that had left their scars on him, but mainly with his own parents. His Dad was military through and through, and while that meant being tough and being dutiful, all things that Will aspired to be himself, it often meant not being there. His Mum had found other ways to occupy her time, and Will had seen how it could all go wrong.

He swore to himself as a young teenager that he'd only ever get married once in his life, and when he did, it would be all or nothing. The only person that had even come close to getting through his defences in the last few years was Lisa, and he found himself having a Woodford moment now. Ready to spill the works.

Thankfully, there was no time, but he swore that before this was over, he'd confide in her. It was the least he should do, she'd saved his arse, just not right now. Now they needed to move.

'Come on. Let's get this bastard before he hurts anyone else.' he said, changing the magazine in his Glock for a fresh one.

'He must still be in the food hall. He's driving them all to the centre' said Lisa, having reached the same conclusions as Will.

'Yeah I figured. That scooter is a fucking mobile bomb. We've got to tread very carefully here Lisa, I think it's a big one.'

The food hall was diagonally opposite the Lush shop. Fifty feet in a straight line, but they couldn't go in a straight line.

There was a mass of people, thousands of them, screaming, crying, shouting for help. They were all pushing and shoving, trying to get into the safety of the great hall. Like the last people in Pompeii, fighting for the high ground, as the land around them is engulfed in flames.

'How the fuck are we going to get in there?' asked Lisa.

'Well, normally I'd say letting off a few rounds would scatter them, but that won't help here. That'll just panic them more and they'll push harder.'

Will did a full three-sixty, looking for something, anything that would give them another way in.

'Hang on a minute. Fuck! Fuck! Fuck!' Will looked like he was having convulsions, his body visibly shaking, dropping his heads into his hands as he shouted like he was having the worst headache of his life. 'Lisa, look!' Will straightened and pointed to the large pillar, opposite the entrance to the hall.

Seven feet from the floor there was what looked like a suicide vest. Only it wasn't strapped to a deranged Jihadi, this one was stuck to the pillar itself. Will traced the structure above the pillar. It looked like a primary support for the entire concourse ceiling. The pillar went all the way to the roof three storeys above them. Each of the floors above had main support beams feeding to the pillar itself.

It that came down, both upper floors would come crashing down, along with this section of the roof too. Thousands of tons of rubble and glass. Thousands of fragile people waiting to cushion it's fall below.

'Shit. Now what?' asked Lisa, seeing what had given Will the sudden headache.

'Let's just play it through. If this all comes down, it'll wipe out all these people, but what about the ones in the hall? I assume the doors on the other side of there are blocked somehow.'

'They'd be trapped.' Agreed Lisa.

'Trapped in an open space with an improvised vehicle bomb. No way out.' Will summarised.

'Wait. How is HE getting out?' asked Lisa, trying to think beyond just the carnage that was unfolding.

'Maybe he's not.' Will thought this was perfectly viable.

'No' said Lisa. 'He's the man behind this. He wouldn't throw himself on his sword. That's not how these sick fucking cowards work. The have their Jihadis for that, their minions, they don't sacrifice the brains when there are plenty of others to do that for them.'

Will saw no harm in running with that as a theory, especially as Al-Naswari would be the brains that was looking to escape, not Aman. 'OK let's say you're right, so how would he get out?'

'The doorways are out of the question. No way through there, certainly for a guy his size. There must be another way. A service door or something.'

Will glanced up and down the concourse. 'I can't see anything from here. We'll have to go out and look.'

They headed out of the shop, keeping left against the cover of the shops once more. The noise from the panicking crowd echoed around the building, making it hard to hear anything, even as close as they were. The crowd was bigger than they first thought, it was blocking the entire walkway ahead.

There was no way to see if there were any service doors or hatches on the other side of the concourse with all those people in the way.

Will leaned back to shout into Lisa's ear 'I've got to let a couple of rounds off, just to get these people to move.'

'OK do it.'

Will raised his weapon, turned back to face Lisa, and pointed it up and away from the crowd, trying to decide where to aim, careful to avoid hitting the pillar and the vest attached to it. Before he could make up his mind there was a burst of gunfire from further down the concourse, behind the crowds of shoppers. Followed by another. And another. They were three-round bursts, it was an MP5, just like the one Will had dropped before Lisa reached him, and the one Neil still had. One person firing.

Will hoped Neil was OK, but he couldn't worry about that now. The crowd was moving away from the gunfire, swarming towards Will and Lisa and away from Lush on the other side. People packed themselves tightly in to the right-hand side of the concourse, taking cover behind each other rather than risk being in the way of a bullet themselves.

That survival instinct, ruthless as it was, created a gap down the left side of the walkway for Will and Lisa to get through, and they didn't hang about.

They got past the crowd just in time to see a service door swinging closed next to the left-hand entry to the food hall. 'There!' shouted Lisa, pointing to the door. She scanned the concourse looking for Aman. A few people were heading away from the food court but none of them were their man, all were far too slim. It was reasonable that others had figured out there was another way out and had taken it, but that only served to make her sure it was the right door.

They ran across the walkway to catch the door before it closed. It could only be opened from the inside, and they didn't want any more delays. Will got their first and stuck his foot in the way of the closing door.

Both took a second to catch their breath, reloading their weapons instinctively. They nodded to each other to signal they were ready, then ducked inside, weapons drawn and ready.

CHAPTER 40 – AMAN ALI

'Time to go.' Aman whispered to himself. He pushed his way through the crowd, easy for a man his size, he brushed people aside like he was parting curtains. Nobody paid much mind to it, they were all being pushed and shoved around, as more and more people forced their way into the hall.

Aman got to the Burger King outlet and walked around the counter. He headed through the kitchen, towards the service door that he knew was there, covered by a large wheeled shelving unit that he'd had Imran place there earlier in the day, under the pretence of a fire hazard test that he was running. That ensured that none of the staff moved it before it was needed.

When he reached the shelving, he stopped and checked behind him, making sure nobody had followed. It was clear, nobody could see him. There was little time. He had to strip down quickly. Kicking off his shoes, ripping off his shirt, unzipping his trousers. It was undignified. His size made it awkward and there wasn't much space. It would've made for a strange sight if anyone had been around. Once his clothes were off, the picture got even more strange. The fat suit that he'd been wearing since he first came to England was brown in colour, only a few shades off his natural skin colour. It was secured in place with large Velcro straps around the stomach, thighs, calves, shoulders, and elbows.

Nobody in the U.K. had known who he really was. The five identity changes that he'd gone through, since being known as Hamza Al-Naswari, the last of his names to come close to being known to security services in Afghanistan, limited the possibility of a connection to his current persona, Aman Ali.

It was easy to change identity when you moved around the Middle East like he had. His connections with Al-Qaeda made it easy to find the resources that he needed. Every time he arrived in a new country, his first task was to burn his current passport and source a new one. Others that he worked with in the past had gotten their new papers just *before* moving on, but he knew that was a mistake. There were ways of tracking passport use. To him it was much better that his identity should disappear from the world the *first* time he used it officially.

The suit had been an extension of Hamza's own body for years. He had completely immersed himself in this identity, he became Aman, and his size was the thing that defined his identity. Undoing the straps and tugging the suit down off his body, Al-Naswari was shedding more than just an elaborate two-hundred-pound disguise, he was becoming himself again. The final part was to remove the full, heavy beard that had been secured to his face with adhesive tape. Removing it was painful, like tearing a plaster from his skin.

All things considered he didn't think he'd use this kind of disguise again. The effort that it took to maintain was exhausting. Every morning and night he had to shave to prevent his facial hair from growing underneath the tape. That was only a small element of the challenge. The physical demands that carrying that extra weight, day in and day out, made on his body were excruciating. He had always been physically muscular, weighing two hundred and twenty pounds in his socks, but even so the toll it took was huge.

His only respite from the suffocating suit came when he showered. In the early days he'd sometimes taken a gamble and removed it when he slept. Sleeping in separate bedrooms to his wife made the deceit easier to hide, but it wasn't a peaceful sleep on those nights. Although he was confident his wife would obey him, and stay out of his room, there was always the risk that she might come in unannounced at any point. After a week of restless sleep, he decided the discomfort of the suit was preferable to the risk of being exposed. After a while he conditioned himself to the situation. He'd never be able to move quickly as Aman, but he could tolerate that.

He'd had to register with a doctor in another part of the city altogether, so that he could abandon the suit should he ever need to seek medical help. The façade was useful as a disguise, but the best doctors in the world would struggle to get a blood pressure reading through Aman's padded arms.

Once the suit, and persona, had been stripped away fully, Al-Naswari kicked it all to one side and put his shoes back on. He had already been dressed in jeans and T-shirt under the suit. He felt free, but cold. He'd been wearing so many layers for so long that wearing only one layer now, along with the air caressing his clean-shaven face, felt alien to him.

Looking down at the discarded suit and clothes, like a butterfly observing the broken husk of a caterpillar's cocoon, Al-Naswari smiled.

'As-Salaam-Alaikum Brother Aman.'

He rolled the shelving unit to one side and pushed through the service door behind. There was a short corridor that lead behind the various kitchen units. He headed left, towards the exit on to the concourse. As he pushed through the door, he saw to his left the crowd were still pushing their way in to the hall. Exactly as he'd planned.

Having now seen both inside and outside the hall, Al-Naswari thought there must be close to 150,000 people in the melee. This was going to be the single biggest blow dealt to the infidel, far surpassing everything that had gone before, and it was all down to him. For once he would get the glory in his own name. He knew that the video streams were going out, he'd checked on his phone before leaving the hall.

At least two of his men were dead already. Their cameras were streaming motionless pictures of the ceiling and floors above. Two more were either dead or had broken cameras, their streams were not showing anything. Hopefully only broken, but if not, there were at least two more still streaming live. He had heard shots still being fired as he made his way through the kitchen. They were still having their fun before the end game.

The final part of the Brothers' mission was to hold back from the food hall. If any police or first responders managed to get access, before the hall went up, then they were to engage and take them out. Hamza didn't think the police would be getting in any time soon, after such comprehensive destruction of the entryways.

He'd also planted one more camera, on the front of the scooter itself. When he'd parked it facing inwards, he'd pointed the camera to broadcast the crowd huddling for safety in the expanse of the hall. He didn't know if it would survive the blast, but it wouldn't matter. It would be clear that the blast had happened and the image of those many thousands of people, straining to get closer to the machine that would wipe them off the face of the earth, would scorch an image on the world that could never be erased.

Once he was more than a hundred yards away from the hall, he hit send on his phone. The penultimate message he would send on this mission. To Abdul. It read simply; NOW.

CHAPTER 41 – ABDUL

The message from Aman had finally come. It was time. Time to let go of the pain that had consumed his world for what felt like his entire life. Ever since he was a boy, all he had known was sadness and death. Every person he'd ever let hold a place in his heart had died. Not just died, but been killed at the hands of another. Was it possible that Aman was responsible for two of them?

Abdul's mind was swimming. He couldn't think straight. The throbbing pulse in his head was back, and stronger than ever. He felt sick.

The trigger for his vest was in his jacket pocket. He slipped his hand in there, cradling it in his palm. One push of a button and his part would be done. His plan was to be by the pillar when he set it off, to go to paradise as a martyr, to be free of all the anguish.

But would he? What was paradise? He'd never really thought about it. These were his final moments. If he was ever going to think about it, now was the time. If he had his choice, paradise would be him and Emily holding hands as they walked home from school, his mum waiting to hear about his day, and his Dad sitting at the dinner table.

Eric interrupted his thoughts.

'Abby. I swear to you, what I'm telling you is the truth. That man, your Uncle, is using you. He killed your parents, and now he's using you to carry out his dirty work. Look, I don't know what that message said, but I can guess. I can see what it's doing to you. I beg you, please don't do this.'

'It's too late Mr Matthews.'

'No! It's not. It's not. Look over there. *Look!*' Eric pointed over his shoulder to the two terrified young girls. Their eyes watery and bright, reflecting the lights of the store above. 'Abby, *please*, look at my girls.'

Abdul shook his head, tears coming to his own eyes now.

'Abby, look! They are just like her. They even have her personality. They are so sweet, so loving. You watched Emily die...' Eric choked on this sentence '...you were there when that beautiful, precious girl was taken from us *both*. Think how you felt. You know how much better this world was with her in it. Now *you* have the chance to make sure that two little girls, exactly like her, can stay in the world. *Look at them!*' Eric shouted.

Abdul wiped his eyes with the back of his hand, the one still holding his phone. He looked up and across to where Jenny and Carrie were sitting, cuddling each other, heads together, looking across at their Dad and this strange man.

It was their eyes. He hadn't seen it before. They had Emily's eyes. Looking at them now, it was like he was eight years old again. He knew he couldn't do it. He let go of the trigger and removed his hand from his pocket. In that one act of letting go, physically and metaphorically, Abdul felt a relief that he couldn't remember ever feeling before. It was like a thick fog, that had settled over the last years of his life, had suddenly lifted.

In that moment, a memory came rushing back to him and he knew with absolute clarity that Eric was telling him the truth. He was a child again. He was at the bottom of the stairs in their house on Darnhill, listening in through the living room door, and looking through the pockets of the coats hung up on the wall.

The picture. The one of his Mum outside the police station. The policeman in the background. It was Eric.

CHAPTER 42 – WILL & LISA

The corridor was long and narrow. It seemed to run the full length of the food hall, with doors leading into each of the different eateries on the right. The first door had an A4 laminated sign with the Burger King logo on it. The door was ajar, not closed properly by whoever had used it last.

The door opened inwards. Will took a second to let Lisa catch up before he kicked it open and burst through with his gun held out before him. The door slammed into a metal shelving unit, holding trays full of dirty kitchenware ready to be washed, sending it crashing to the ground.

The noise startled Lisa. She hadn't registered the shelving unit as she'd raced in behind Will, and spun round at the sound of the crash. Her feet got caught in something on the ground and she went down hard, landing on her shoulder on the cold floor tiles.

'Fuck!' she muttered angrily, lifting herself on to her elbows. 'What's that?' She gestured to the brown thing, that looked and felt like a beanbag, tangled around her bare feet.

'I don't know. Just get loose of it and let's get moving.' Said Will, scanning the room ahead of them.

'Just wait a minute. Let me see what this thing is. It doesn't belong in here.' Lisa sat up, drawing her feet up to her, dragging the fat suit closer to her. She got to her feet, taking the thing with her. It was heavy. She could bench-press a lot more than her own body weight, it was one of her favourite stations in the gym. She found it rewarding to be able to lift more than some of the men there. Her personal best was one hundred and sixty pounds, not professional weightlifter standard, but certainly better than most women could do. Despite that, she struggled to lift the thing fully off the ground.

'What is it? It smells like an old gym bag, it's disgusting.' she said as a waft of the stale sweat that had built up on the inside of the suit invaded her nostrils.

Attached to one of the Velcro straps, hanging loosely at the side of the suit, was a decent sized beard with strips of adhesive tape still clinging to the back of it. Will dropped his chin to his chest and put his hands on his knees.

'Sneaky bastard!' He said to the floor.

'What?' asked Lisa, unable to hear him clearly with his head down like it was.

'It's a fucking fat suit. He wasn't disguising himself with the scooter, he was disguising himself with *that*!' said Will.

'Oh bollocks!' Said Lisa, realising what a problem this gave them. 'So, what are we actually looking for?'

'I don't know what he looks like now. I've got no fucking idea. But I know *who* he is. Aman Ali IS Hamza Al-Naswari. He's been here the whole time, right under our noses. What the fuck do we do now? We've got no idea what he looks like, except that he's *not* fat. He can detonate that bomb before we even get close to him'

Lisa dropped the foul-smelling suit on the ground. 'Ok, so let's go one step at a time. This was dumped here, so we can assume that he's not in the hall any more, right? He's changed his appearance before heading out of here, so he's out on the concourse somewhere.'

'Yes, let's go. We need to move fast now, once he's clear of the blast radius, everyone in that room is fucked.'

CHAPTER 43 – HAMZA AL-NASWARI

Abdul's pillar was still intact. Something had gone wrong. He fumbled for his phone, walking briskly away from the food hall. As he clicked into his message folder, to make sure that his last had sent, he was stopped in his tracks. A message from Abdul was there waiting for him. Hamza was instantly furious. He had been explicit in his instructions; contact was *only* to be initiated by him. Breaking from the plan was, in his experience, the fastest path to detection.

Normally there would have to be grave punishment for going against instructions, but once Hamza had cleared up whatever last-minute question Abdul had asked in his message, the boy would be no more anyway. Hamza glanced around to make sure he was alone, moving closer to the windows of the shops on his right to limit his exposure, and clicked on the message to open it.

It wasn't a question but a statement. A short, but very powerful statement.

I KNOW WHAT YOU DID. I KNOW ABOUT MY MUM AND MY AUNT, *YOUR OWN WIFE*. I'M OUT. I HOPE THEY CATCH YOU, AND IF THEY DON'T TODAY, THEN I'LL MAKE SURE THEY DO TOMORROW.

How could he possibly know? Who was left that could have told him? These questions were quickly burned away by the fury rising in Hamza's mind. He felt no guilt for the things that he'd done. They were necessary and righteous for his mission. Abdul's would have to be another death added to the list for this betrayal, after this was over. Hamza started walking again, typing a one-handed reply as he did:

YOU KNOW NOTHING BUT I PROMISE YOU SOON WILL. YOUR MOTHER WAS A TRAITOR, SHE PAID A TRAITOR'S PRICE. YOUR FATHER WAS A TRAITOR

TOO AND I MADE SURE THAT HE WAS PUNISHED FOR THAT, JUST LIKE I WILL FOR YOU. YOU DIDN'T KNOW ABOUT THAT, DID YOU? YOU WILL KNOW MUCH MORE WHEN I FIND YOU.

Hamza hit send and, in that action, consigned Abdul to the 'to be dealt with' section of his mind. Back to the plan, he thought, stay focused now. There were still plenty of people packed into the hall, and from what he'd seen, they weren't eager to go back out into the walkways in case there were more shooters out there.

He headed to the Lush shop. Wearing his padded suit, and the extra layers of clothes underneath, had been tough work. His clothes were soaked with sweat, the stench was awful, he could smell it on himself. It was unavoidable, but he'd planned for it. He'd take shelter in Lush and wait to be rescued along with the few other survivors that there were bound to be. There were plenty of things in the shop that he could use to mask the smell in the meantime, and if he remained in there until he was found then the overpowering fragrances of the place would make sure no suspicion fell on him.

He'd had many proud moments, but this part of the plan he thought was a particular stroke of genius, the shop was far enough away from the blast that, once tucked safely away in the storeroom out the back, he'd trigger the scooter.

CHAPTER 44 – WILL & LISA

They burst through the doors back on to the concourse, the noise of them metal crashing in to the wall as the doors swung wildly open making the crowd jump again, thinking they were under fire again.

He couldn't have gone left, Will thought. The crowd had fanned back out, filling the width of the place. He wouldn't be safe to detonate in there, so he must have gone right. They turned that way and ran.

'How will we know it's him?' Lisa shouted to Will, a few feet out in front.

'I don't know. Just look for anyone that's a possible to start with. There aren't many people out here now. They can't all look the same.'

He was right. Ignoring the casualties, which she was trying very hard to do, there were only two people in view. A black woman, on her knees, cradling a bloodied child in her arms, crying, and kissing his head, and a white guy, mid-to-late thirties. He was watching Will, but as far as Lisa could tell was no threat. Besides, she could see that Will had also clocked him. He said something to the guy as he ran past that she couldn't make out. Presumably telling him to stay covered.

As Lisa ran past Lush, her breathing disturbed by the aromatic cloud that acted as the company's logo, she realised how they could identify him.

'Will!' She shouted. 'The smell. We'll know it's him because he'll stink. That suit was foul.'

It took Will a further twenty feet of running to process what Lisa had shouted from behind him. He slammed on the brakes, his feet skidding along the polished floor like a little boy on the dancefloor at a wedding. Lisa was coming up fast behind him, she didn't have time to react and almost wiped him out, leaping to the side of him at the last moment.

'Whoa!' She shouted as she jumped just past his shoulder. 'What are you doing Will?'

'You're right. It's the smell. So, if I smelled like that, I know exactly what I'd do to make sure I wasn't found.'

'What?'

'Look' he said, pointing back the way they came, to the black and white signage above Lush, 'I'd be in there.'

She knew he was right as soon as she saw the shop. It was perfect.

They jogged the thirty feet back to the shop, stopping just short of the window. Will leaned to the side, just enough to get a peek through the glass, to get a view inside. There, at the back of the shop, was a dark-skinned man struggling with a door. As far as Will could see he was unarmed. Presumably, he was holding the detonator for the scooter bomb but in terms of small arms, he seemed to be clean.

It made sense if he was looking to get out of here. It wasn't like he could just walk out the front door. He'd have to hole up until the place was cleared and make out like he was a shopper. Everyone would be thoroughly searched before they'd be allowed to leave, so carrying a weapon would be a bad idea.

Fast and quiet, they entered the shop. They were ten feet behind when Al-Naswari stopped struggling with the door and took his phone out of his pocket.

CHAPTER 45 – HAMZA AL-NASWARI

Plans never went perfectly. Hamza knew that the secret to success, especially on a mission as elaborate as this one, was to cover as many potential points of failure as possible. You always relied on a little good fortune.

The storeroom door was a failure point that he couldn't control. He'd planned to be in there when the blast went off, but someone else had clearly beaten him to it, and had barricaded the door closed behind them. He tried to force it open but couldn't do it.

They probably thought he was one of the shooters, so of course they wouldn't let him in willingly, and he couldn't risk drawing attention to himself by shouting at them to open it. He had to be invisible now that he was no longer Aman. Even though nobody knew who Hamza was, or what he looked like, he felt exposed.

He couldn't wait to get to the airport. He had his new passport in his pocket. It went against all his normal rules to use a brand-new identity on a traceable flight, but on this occasion, he was willing to do something different.

He only planned on keeping this one for as long as it took to get out of the U.K. He'd already been recommended a forger that could get him more papers when he landed. Rashad Ahmed: English teacher, charity worker and passionate pianist, was going to exist for a mere matter of hours, the first act of his life being to board a flight to Morocco, and the last passing through Moroccan border control.

Until then he just had to stay under the radar. There was one last thing to do, and he was sure he'd be just as safe from the blast in the main area of the shop. The storeroom would be better but was probably unnecessary.

He stepped back from the door and reached into his pocket for his phone. The detonator on his scooter was just one click away.

CHAPTER 46 – WILL & LISA

They didn't say anything. Didn't shout "Freeze" or "Stop, police", that stuff only happened on T.V. In real life, you didn't give anybody a head-start like that.

Was this it? Was he hitting the trigger?

They couldn't wait to find out. Will fired. Two shots, low, so as not to hit the trigger itself. Both slugs found the meat in the back of Al-Naswari's right thigh, spinning him to the left and down to the deck.

The pair closed on him quickly, looking for the trigger. It was still in his hand.

'Don't do it!' Shouted Lisa 'Your only hope is to give up that detonator right now.'

No, no, no. What are you doing Lisa? Will's mind was racing. He hadn't come this far and taken these risks, only for Al-Naswari to be arrested. No way was this fucker going to HMP All-Inclusive, he killed Luke. He'd killed at least a hundred people here today, and he wasn't finished yet, he still had the trigger in his hand and could finish the job. Trying to talk him down at this point was madness. Surely, she could see that? Surely, after everything Al-Naswari had done here today, without even knowing what else he'd done, she wanted to put a bullet in him as badly as Will did?

Fuck! He thought. What now? If she tries to take him alive, what can I do? I don't know. I'll have to think of something. I can't let him live, I just can't.

Will glanced sideways at Lisa, his heart racing 'We can't risk it, we've got to take him out now. No more warnings.'

'I know,' said Lisa, 'I just did that for the paperwork.' as she raised her gun again. Will's hadn't lowered.

She had no intention of taking this animal in alive. Not after what she'd seen today. She was tough. She could handle anything. Or so she thought. Running through the walkways of this centre today, seeing those children killed, maimed, orphaned, lying bleeding, and broken hearted and scared, had changed her.

Anyone that was capable of that had to die. Simple.

Hamza spotted the pause, the indecision, he smiled and moved his thumb 'Allahu A...'

He didn't finish his sentence. He didn't finish his plan. Six rounds tore through his chest, head, and stomach almost simultaneously. Destroying his heart and his brain in the same moment.

CHAPTER 47 – AFTERMATH

Nobody could leave the shopping centre until everyone had been thoroughly checked out. Chief Atkinson had decided it was best to clear the building in sections, to avoid having so many people all trying to leave at once.

He ran the operation well. It needed an academic brain to co-ordinate the whole thing. They started in the food hall. Punching through the door there was the easiest way in and was the option that the tactical team had eventually opted for. The roof was just not secure enough. Besides, there were still two explosives to deal with and that had to be the priority.

The initial body count was already above three hundred, with one section of the building still to be cleared. It would have been many more if the scooter had gone up. The bomb squad tech that dismantled it suggested it would have taken upwards of ten thousand, possibly as high as twenty. Another two thousand or more if the last pillar had also gone. They wouldn't have had a final number until after weeks of sifting the wreckage.

In total eight terrorists had been confirmed dead. Two on the west mall and two at the junction with the east mall were shot and killed by SO15 officers on site. One was killed in the security control room by an SO15 officer. Another two had been found shot dead in the East mall. It was unclear who was responsible for that. The working theory was that they had an altercation and had shot each other. The last, confirmed as the leader of the group, Aman Ali, AKA Hamza Al-Naswari, had also been killed by SO15 officers.

After detailed background checks were performed on shoppers wanting to leave the centre, only one person of interest was flagged. Abdul Azim. He was the nephew by marriage of Aman Ali.

It took three hours, but a statement from Eric Matthews, a serving police officer, cleared Abdul. He had been shopping with Matthews. The boy and Matthews' daughter Emily had been together when she was killed in the Arndale bombing. The two had stayed close ever since. Matthews was a respected officer, in charge of cadet recruitment, and his statement was, eventually, enough to clear Azim.

Will hadn't seen Neil since they'd caught Al-Naswari. He'd told him to play dumb and get out safely when he ran past him in the mall earlier and could only assume that's what he had done. By now he must have been cleared to leave. With the cameras offline, there was nothing to connect him to anything. Thankfully, that meant there was also no evidence of his own illegal activities either.

That didn't take away the guilt he felt about lying to Lisa, leaving her in danger. He hung around waiting for her to be cleared by the paramedics.

'Drink?' he asked, 'I know a pub nearby with a great jukebox and a free pool table.' He handed her the Michael Kors shoes that he'd gone back to collect from the control room, knowing that she wouldn't leave until they were safely back on her feet.

'You're buying.' She said, slipping her feet back in to the heels.

'Deal.' He said, and they headed out of the food hall door.

'Shit! The car is all the way around the other side of the bloody building.' Complained Will.

'Oh well. At least we're outdoors, and It's not raining,' said Lisa, 'plus, a good walk will give you plenty of time to tell me about your mate.'

'What mate?'

'The one who speaks hand signal. You were behind me, stupid. I saw your reflection in the Ann Summers shop window.'

Will stopped walking and gawped at Lisa. She thought he looked like a slack-jawed idiot, or a Yorkshireman, as they were called around here. 'Not a good look Will, pick your chin up.' She laughed. 'Come on, you can't get a meat pie past me, did you really think I wouldn't pick up on this?'

'Well, I had hoped, yes! Look, Lisa, I feel awful about lying to you. I'm sorry. It's a very long story though.'

'I've got all night. But just so you know I refuse to share my bed with a man that is hiding something from me. So, unless you want to risk me getting hangry again, you'll summarise!'

She knew that what he'd done had not been by the book. But she knew the man. He wouldn't go so far off-script, unless there was a genuine reason and she had time to think about it while she was in the back of the ambulance, waiting for the paramedic to tell her what she already knew, she was fine. After today, whatever Will was going to tell her didn't matter. She trusted him. More than any other partner she'd had before.

She thought back to how she had felt when she had Al-Naswari in her gun sights today. In her mind she had weighed up the carnage that he had caused and, in that moment, made her decision. All her training, all the rules, had gone out of the window. She'd given the warning, not for the paperwork or because that's what her training told her to do, but to test Will, and see what his reaction would be.

Pulling the trigger without saying a word would've been what she'd done had he not been there with her, but she needed to be sure he'd side with her. It turned out they were aligned in more ways than she'd realised, and she was very happy about that.

She winked at him and slipped her arm through his to walk a bit closer. She might just love him. It was a thought that had been hiding in that shadowy corner of her mind, the place where the brain puts things when you're not quite ready to accept them. For her, this thought had showed itself properly for the first time today, as she was running through the building looking for him.

There was no way she'd tell Will about that, at least until he'd said it to her first. She'd gone this long without saying anything, and could go much longer if needed.

She hoped she wouldn't have to though.

CHAPTER 48 – THE BRIMSONS

Karen was going to pee herself if they didn't let her out of here soon. It was alright for Simon and Josh, they peed in the corner of the storeroom while they were stuck in there. It wasn't so easy for her though, and Sophie *definitely* wouldn't. Teenagers were teenagers, no matter what was going on around them.

Now that it was over, Josh was having a whale of a time. There were police, fire engines, ambulances, everywhere you looked. Lots of men with guns, but they were the good guys so that was OK.

Josh wasn't happy that Spiderman had been and gone already, but at least he'd heard him bashing the bad guys that had come into the shop looking for people. He knew that Spidey didn't normally shoot guns, but he didn't suppose it mattered, if he won. Before he'd got there, the bad guy had tried to open the door, but his Mum and Dad had put all their weight on the boxes to stop anyone getting in.

Dad said that they'd even shot guns through the door, but that the candles had stopped the bullets. Mum said that she was buying more candles from there from now on.

Simon couldn't wait to get home. Not just because he was tired, and really needed a beer, but once the kids were safely in bed, he was going to enjoy giving Karen the "I told you so" speech. He was very excited.

CHAPTER 49 - ABDUL

'I don't understand Mr Matthews. Why did you do that? You risked your job, you risked everything.' Abby asked from the passenger seat. The last message he'd got from his Uncle had put his brain in a spin. He had gone into his own head, replaying his entire life in his mind, trying to make sense of it all. This had probably saved him in the end. He had been desperate for someone to tell him what to do, so when Eric had given him a script to stick to with the police, he absorbed it easily and stuck to it word for word. Eric stayed by his side throughout.

Eric signalled to come off the M62 at Birch services. They were nearly home now.

'I've had a long time to think Abby. That day at the Arndale, I could've risked my job and come out of that car park to make sure that Emily was safe. I didn't. Because of that, I never got to hold my baby again. The way I see it, I owed my baby a big risk. What better way to repay her, than helping you? I know you Abby, maybe not one to one like we are now, but my Emily couldn't half talk. "Abby, Abby, Abby," was all we ever heard in our house for a long time. She talked about you a lot, and you can come to know someone well when you hear so much about them. I know how you tried to protect her, I know you loved her, and I know you'd have never hurt her.'

'No sir, I wouldn't.'

'So that's how I also know that, whatever was happening today, it wasn't really you. I'm sorry that I didn't get to you before now about your Uncle. In my book that means that I owe you too. You'll stay with us until we figure out what's next ok?'

'I think you've already repaid that debt Mr Matthews.' Said Abby.

'Eric, please. And no, I haven't, not just yet. Listen Abby. The world has changed. Attacks like this are the biggest risk that we face nowadays. It might not be on the news all the time but it's always there. We could use someone with your experience to help us fight that. Not now of course, but how do you feel about joining the force and doing that Son?'

EPILOGUE

The seats were amazing. Stretford End, second row, right behind the goal. Abby couldn't believe he was finally at a United game after all this time. Shame he'd missed their best years, but he had a good feeling about the transfer window coming up. If they could just get a couple of decent midfielders and defenders in, they could stick it to City next year.

Eric was enjoying the game too. He was a City fan himself, but not one of the knobhead ones. He appreciated a good game, whoever was playing. Abby had promised that, as a thank you to Eric for helping him get into the force, and for his support throughout the probationary process, he was going to take him to a *real* game of football.

It had taken a while. United tickets were bloody hard to get hold of, but finally here they were, United versus West Brom, no less than ten months since he'd passed his probation. It wasn't a glamour game by any stretch, but a tough one for sure. It was cold, it was raining, and Pogba still couldn't hit a cow's arse with a banjo, but Abby was happy. He liked the rain. It felt like home.

It was good timing too. Now that Abby had passed all his training, he was about to move into a new unit. Eric's new unit. He'd got the ball rolling to set it up when he returned to the force after Emily had died. Abby had been selected based on several things: His unique experience firstly. He had a level of insight that few people in the world had. He had lived with Hamza Al-Naswari for years. He knew all the people that met with him and had witnessed everything possible about the man. Nobody else on earth could say they had the same experience.

His skin colour and background were the second. He wasn't offended by this, a lot of people might be, but to him it was a just a tool to be used and now he had a reason to use it. Outside of Hamza there was a variety of people and organisations that represented a threat to the people of the U.K.

It just happened that Abby would be able to fit in physically with most of them.

Eric had successfully deprogrammed Abby over the course of a year. Abby didn't know what deprogramming was in a technical sense, he defined it as showing a consistent level of care and love that he'd not had since he was a kid. Abby was excited about the future. He had a purpose. To stop any other children going through what he had. He was determined to do exactly that.

Eric's new unit was an undercover one, proactively targeting potential extremist threats. After the recent incidents at the Trafford Centre, as well as at the Ariana Grande concert shortly before, the Commissioner of Greater Manchester Police had been all too keen to take action, he happily gave Eric the sign off he needed to set up the joint task force with SO15. Eric had pitched the idea to the Commissioner some time ago and, after everything he knew about the boy, had handpicked Abby to be the first recruit.

There were a few people that Eric had introduced Abby to over the past three months, that had also been earmarked for the new undercover unit. Abby knew they all had their own versions of his personal story, although he was sure they were probably not as eventful as his own. He'd get to know their stories in time, for now, it was just good to have friends again. He'd hit it off with one of them right from the word go.

In fact, he was meeting him for a beer and a game of pool later that night. His new friend, Neil Green, was a bit intense, he was the only guy Abby knew, besides himself, that came close to having what they called in the films a "thousand-yard stare". He seemed like a good guy though, and Abby was happy to meet up with him, to get a bit of a social life going again.

It wasn't just a catch up this time though. Neil had text Abby earlier that day to say he wanted to meet up, that he wanted to get something off his chest, and only Abby would understand.

From the Author

This is my first book, so if you've managed to get this far then thank you for persevering and seeing it through.

If you've enjoyed it, I would be forever grateful if you would leave a review on Amazon, Audible, or wherever else you may have found it.

I'm learning quickly that a good review is worth far more than anything else when it comes to helping other readers find my work. There's a link below for ebook readers, for any paperback readers, please go to the page that you ordered from and choose to leave a review.

Incognito - Leave a review

Thank you.

This is a work of fiction. I've borrowed parts of names from those I love, with their blessing, as a way of honouring them, but the story and characters themselves are entirely the product of imagination.

I am under no illusion that this is a masterpiece of any kind, but I am hoping that by putting it out there I can learn. The decision to release this book now was a tough one. I'm technically not ready to publish yet. There's a lot more scrutiny, and procrastination, to be done and even now I'm finding bits that I want to change. That, I'm starting to understand, will likely always be the case.

More importantly though I've taken the decision now because we're in a very strange world right now. As I'm writing this, we're in the middle of the Coronavirus lockdown. The UK has been shut down officially for just over a week, the Prime Minister is isolated in a flat above Downing Street, and there's been no football for weeks, possibly there won't be again this season.

That's the hardest part for me as an avid United fan. This whole strange situation got me thinking that perhaps I should release it now. If I can contribute even slightly to making this odd time a little lighter for anyone, that is worth far more than my constant editing.

When I'm not dreaming of becoming a full-time author; sitting by my window, typing, and indulging my delusions, I work in financial services. A very different world indeed, but one that I'm thankfully pretty good at (something needs to cover the costs for this hobby of mine!).

I am a proud father of 4 and a very happily married man. My wife, Lisa, is not sure yet if she loves her namesake in Incognito or if she hates me for, in her words, making her a bit slutty! The answer to that will most likely be linked to the amount of people that end up reading it.

Thank you again for reading on. I deeply appreciate it and I hope to hear from you with what you would like to see change or develop in this story as well as any ideas you may have for how Lisa, Will and Abby might move forward from here. I have my own ideas of course, but if you have listened to me for this long then it's only right and fair that I should listen to you before forcing my will on you!

I hope to speak to you again very soon. In the meantime you can find out more about what's coming next at www.michaelwinson.com

Stay safe

Michael Winson

Lisa, Will, Neil and Abby will return very soon.